Unhinged
TITAN

E.V. OLSEN

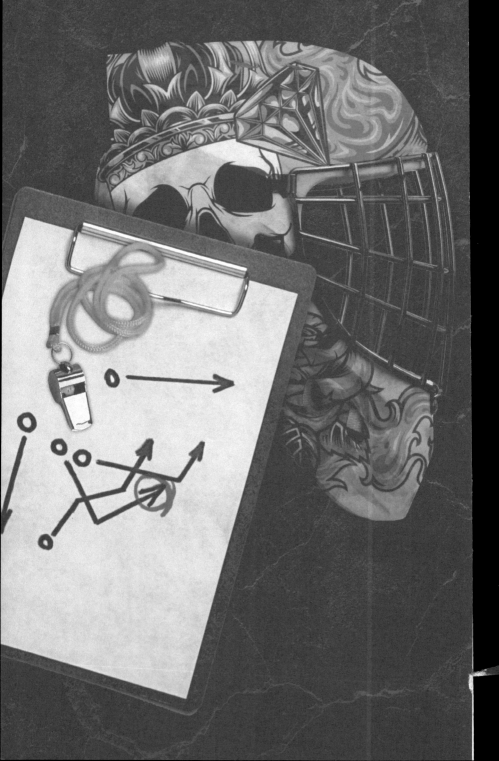

Tropes and Trigger
WARNINGS

Tropes

COACH/PLAYER, AGE GAP, FORBIDDEN/
OFF-LIMITS, POSSESSIVE/PROTECTIVE MCS,
OBSESSIVE/POSSESSIVE/PROTECTIVE MCS,
TOUCH HIM AND DIE, SECRET RELATIONSHIP,
STALKER MC, MASKED MC

Trigger Warnings

THIS BOOK CONTAINS SOME THEMES THAT MAY
BE DISTRESSING TO READERS INCLUDING:
DESCRIPTIVE SEX SCENES, IMPACT PLAY,
VIOLENCE, ROUGH SEXUAL PLAY, CANNIBALISM,
BULLYING, MENTION OF INCEST, MURDER,
MENTION OF PAST ANIMAL ABUSE, PET
BEING PUT IN DANGER (BUT IS SAVED),
STALKING, DUBCON,
QUESTIONABLE POWER DYNAMIC

Viktor

CHAPTER ONE

Soft music fills the expansive circular room that sits on the upper level of the mega-yacht. As we step inside, the glass surrounding us showcases all the stars bedazzling the ink-black sky. I strut in first, a broad smile on my face. "Your king has arrived."

Of course that garners some chuckles, then handshakes. Nothing like being the adored goalie of the Crestwood University Titans hockey team.

Feisty Mouse nudges my shoulder. "Do you always need to be the center of attention?"

I snort. "I'm the damn sun, center of the universe."

"The sun is not the center of the universe." Zach adjusts that ugly ass pink gold Audemars Piguet watch of his.

Who even gets pink gold?

Now, my cobalt blue watch, complete with glare proof sapphire crystals from their Royal Oak collection, makes a statement.

Alexei wraps his big lug arm over Eli, then pulls him away, and my smile fades. Sure, I get it. They want to spend as much time together as they can since Alexei signed with the New Jersey Devils. But those fucknuts left me alone most of the summer to go to *Minnesota*.

Nothing like having my cousin and best friend ditch me to go see the Feisty Mouse family. Well, Alexei also did some offseason training while out there. But they could've invited me along.

Can't be too mad. I'm proud of my cousin and happy the NHL finally took notice of him. It'll be weird not having him around, but he's leaving Eli in my care so at least I'll still have my best friend.

Of course, Jackson's outside talking to Killian. Curious what this season's going to be like when we play the Serpents. But those two consider fighting a type of foreplay, so the games will probably continue to be just as intense.

I'm worried about him though. We haven't met our new assistant coach yet, and while my teammate claims he's fine, I notice little details that say otherwise. They're easy to spot since we're roommates this year. Not that he has to worry. He has us, and if this new guy is an issue . . . we'll take care of him.

Connor slaps my shoulder. "Time to schmooze."

My favorite pastime activity—being the center of attention, and the Annual Gala hosted by Crestwood's Department of Athletics is the perfect opportunity.

To my left, Zach's eyes blaze, his fists clench and, to be blunt, he looks like he's about to murder someone. While I love attention, he barely enjoys being around the five of us. Things between him and me were awkward for a while after the one time we played together.

Didn't know what I was getting into, how sadistic he can get. Unfortunately, scars were left. Think Zach's secretly afraid of what Alexei would do if he finds out.

Not that I'd ever tell my cousin.

But over the summer, Zach came to me for help. Turns out, he needs my assistance in tracking down that cockroach of a stepbrother he has. A specialty of mine, thanks to my mother and her family.

Sure, the larger part of the family business is definitely not legal. But we're powerful. And matriarchal.

Thank God.

At least I never have to worry about giving up hockey. My sister, on the other hand, lives with my aunt, Alexei's mom, who runs the show and is training her to take over one day.

Mom and Dad made sure I'm capable of taking care of myself too. They taught me how to protect myself, along with other skills that feed into my stalker tendencies.

Stupid them.

But thanks to their not-so-bright idea, I spent most of the summer trying to help my teammate track down his runaway sibling.

Turns out, the little shit nearly killed Zach five years ago, and my friend is hellbent on ending his existence.

The chatter in the room grows louder as more people arrive. Connor and I spend a good half an hour mingling with the donors. More like practicing our manipulation skills. And damn am I good.

When our team captain starts flirting with some girl, I make my way to the lounge area, then drop into a chair next to Zach, who's scrolling through his phone. "If I can pretend I'm straight, can't you pretend to have emotions?"

"Emotions are overrated. And, unlike you, I don't need the attention." His tone is as cold and flat as ever. It's like talking to a wall sometimes, but that's just Zach.

"Blah, blah." I sit farther back into the soft, leather chair. "Haven't pinpointed your little cockroach yet."

"Neither has my father's private investigator. Just find that little fuck first."

I nod as I take in the room, my attention settling on a man at the bar. He's cute with his thick, dark brown hair that's shorter on the sides and longer on top. And the way his trimmed beard frames his jawline is making my dick hard.

Love the whole rugged yet refined appearance. Goes well with that tousled style he's got going on.

Effortless yet meticulously groomed.

My head tilts, and I look closer at the way he glances around and hunches over, as if he doesn't belong.

And that suit . . . cheap. Well, cheap for this crowd.

Yep. He's not supposed to be here.

Bet the fucktard snuck on the yacht. Or maybe he's one of these rich ole ladies' side pieces.

Too bad. He's making my dick twitch, so he's mine now. "Time to have some fun."

Zach glances up from his phone. "Don't kill anyone. None of our fathers will be able to save your ass."

"Yeah, yeah. Time and place. Heard it before." I wave a haphazard hand, then straighten my Brioni suit jacket, eye-fucking my toy for the night.

The man's swirling his near empty glass of whatever, so I take the opportunity to lean against the bar sideways, staring right at him. "Need another?"

"I'm good." He doesn't bother looking up and it sends a jolt through me.

A challenge.

"Man of few words. I like it." I signal the bartender. "Macallan 26 neat. Another on the rocks."

After showing her my ID, she goes about getting our drinks.

"Said I was good."

"You're milking ice water at this point. Just say thank you and stop being so grumpy. It's a gala."

He snorts.

"Care to tell me how you snuck onto the yacht? You obviously don't belong here."

The grump of a man turns, glaring at me, and holy fuck he's one of those people with two different eye colors—one green and one blue.

"You're so pretty."

The words slip out. Not that I wanted to stop them, but I certainly didn't voluntarily say them.

Not even sure why the fuck that turns me on. Maybe because I've only seen it in movies. Bet it'll be a sight to behold when I'm on my knees, staring up into them with his dick stuffed in my mouth.

His face softens a bit, the side of his mouth twitching as if he wants to smile but fights it.

The bartender brings our drinks and I pick up my glass, taking a sip. "So, which of these old hags brought you along? Or was I right the first time?"

And now he's impassive once again. Swear it's like talking to Zach.

He gets up, then walks away. From me. Leaving the fucking thousand-dollar glass of whiskey on the bar.

Fine, the money I can wipe my ass with. His attitude, on the other hand, is clouding my normally sunshiny—and slightly unhinged—personality.

I turn to the bartender and throw down three thousand dollars, wink, then follow after him with my drink in hand.

Up ahead, he stops and talks to Coach Nieminen, so I hang back. Coach Fuckhead will start lecturing me about drinking. Like that's the worst thing I've done. Bet most of his gray hairs are from me and my friends.

Although, there's that dark streak that runs through him too.

We suspected it at first, but when he helped drug Coach Buckland after he beat the shit out of Jackson we knew. Like it was no sweat off his back.

What did he say? Oh, yeah. *"He's no more valuable than the bag of trash I throw out every Sunday."*

I chuckle, a bit too loudly, then duck behind a group of old geezers to stay hidden.

They talk for a while, and it occurs to me my new toy didn't sneak onto the mega-yacht. He was invited. But it's obvious he doesn't want to be here.

Too bad.

His loss is my dick's gain.

Eventually, he makes his way to the bathroom, and taking a page out of Alexei's book, I follow a few minutes later. While I might be unhinged, I draw the line at flirting with guys as they take a leak.

Only because I did it once, and the fucker must've eaten asparagus or some shit because his piss stank. Gave me the instant ick.

I look at my Audemars Piguet. Five minutes should be long enough to have finished. I saunter down the hallway, then into the expansive marble bathroom.

Crestwood University spares no expense when it comes to the athletics fundraiser. Then again, they have no choice. No one would come if they got some ratty-ass party boat.

"And there he is, the man of the hour." I walk over, sip my drink, then place the glass down.

He stares at me by way of the mirror as he washes his hands.

I flash a grin, flipping my wavy blond hair from my eyes. "Oh, come on now. I know you love my sunny disposition."

He just shakes his head, still indifferent.

I sigh dramatically. "Let me guess, you're straight."

"What I am is of no concern to you."

Some other guest comes out of the stall and washes his hands. I quirk a brow and the fucker snickers. But I catch the way this jackass casually splays his fingers and graze's my toy's ass on his way out.

Wrong move, fuckface.

When the idiot gets closer, I grab his hair and smash his face into the wall. Well, more accurately, the full-length mirror attached to the wall. "Didn't they teach you in school to keep your hands to yourself?"

He yelps as blood runs down his nose, covering his lips and chin.

"What the hell is wrong with you?"

I ignore my toy and shove the perv toward the door. "Say you fell. Otherwise, you'll be swimming back to shore—if you even make it."

The man grabs a shit ton of paper towels, then runs out. I turn back to my toy, pick up my glass, then hold it up and give an air-cheer. "You're welcome."

"You're insane."

I sip my whiskey, then place the glass back down. "Yeah, but I *am* your knight in shining armor."

He keeps that indifferent expression as he tries to step around me, but I move in front of him. "You're really not going to say thank you?"

"For what?"

"Did you want him to touch your ass?"

He doesn't answer.

"Did you?"

"No."

I curtsey and grin. "Hence, your knight in shining armor."

"Grow up." He places a hand on my chest, moving me forcefully, yet carefully—if that's even possible—out of the way, then pulls the door open and walks out.

Okay, so that didn't necessarily go the way I wanted, but he didn't run screaming from me like most people do.

That's a plus. And I can be *mature*.

I look in the mirror, adjust some wavy strands of hair, straighten my suit jacket, then grab my glass and head out.

Whoever this guy is, he's stuck on the yacht with me for the rest of the night. Plenty of time to win him over.

Viktor

My spotlight-stealing performance was the talk of campus for weeks after we won the Frozen Four championship. People who are normally afraid of me smiled and uttered congratulations. Some were even brazen enough to ask for fist bumps.

"Better get it in gear Novy. You don't want to be late your first day back," Connor says.

He's back in captain mode.

Pulling my sweatshirt over my head, I take a second to readjust my pelvic protector, then reach for my goalie pants. "Wonder who our new assistant coach will be."

Connor runs some clear tape over his socks and shin guards. "Heard the university took care of it this time. No parental input."

Jackson flinches.

It's not his fault his dad recommended some homophobe piece of shit. But those sharks were well fed, so at least something came out winning.

Being my friend is still sensitive over what happened, I keep my mouth shut. For once. Only because Eli read me the riot act for sending a shark bait meme in the group chat.

"Think he knows the drill?" I pull on my chest protector, velcroing the straps snugly. "You know, about keeping out of our business."

"Coach Nieminen will make sure this new dick will get with the program." Zach smirks as he tightens his laces.

Speaking of Satan, Coach Nieminen strides into the locker room. "Asses on the ice in four minutes or else."

I give a salute, then blow him a kiss. His fingers tighten around the clipboard in his hand and I'm sure he'd love to smash the thing over my head. But I know the truth—he'll miss me when I graduate.

Though he can always watch me on TV since the Islanders are still interested in signing me.

Once I'm ready, the four of us make our way out to the rink. I've missed the familiar chill of the ice as it permeates the air. Jackson and I talk as we skate to the bench when Zach bumps my shoulder.

"This season should be fun for you." He juts his chin toward Coach Nieminen and . . .

No fucking way.

Jackson eyes Zach. "Who's he?"

"The guy Novy was trying to fuck at the gala."

I don't miss the way he says *trying*, because for the rest of the night the guy from the bar evaded me.

Me.

The one with the best stalking skills of all time. There's a reason I'm the go to when it comes to intel. But this asshole made me all gloomy instead of the ray of psychotic sunshine I normally am.

Payback's a bitch and I'm here to collect.

I pull off my helmet and flip back my blonde waves. "Long time no see, hot stuff."

If looks could kill, I'd be vaporized right now.

"Hope you have extra Motrin on you. He's a handful." Coach Nieminen pins me with a glare next. "Novotny, keep the antics to a minimum this season. We've got a title to defend."

"Oh, I'm definitely worth the headaches I cause." I smile extra wide, then wink at our new assistant coach.

Coach Nieminen pinches the bridge of his nose and shakes his head while Kyle Rinne, my goalie coach, places a hand over his mouth to hide his laughter. But the way his shoulders shake, it's obvious. Love the guy. He puts up with me without complaining.

Mostly.

Seems only when I talk excessively does he ever groan, but that has to do with his kid. Met the boy once, and let me tell you, he can outtalk me ten times over.

"This is Beckett Harper, our new assistant coach, formally with Tampa Bay." Nieminen turns to face Walsh. "He's been caught up on *all* the team's history."

Connor nods.

Of course Nieminen lets Beckett run practice today, as if it's some sort of audition. And this fucker grinds us into the ice. Even makes me participate instead of working with Rinne.

I thought I was in shape. Wrong. I can't catch my damn breath. There's so much sweat in my gear, it's as if I jumped into a lake.

Beckett Harper has once again turned me gloomy. But my smile returns when he blows a long whistle that signals the end of practice.

"Thanks for the workout, Becks."

"It's Coach Harper."

Oh, this is going to be fun. He doesn't realize it yet, but he's already mine. I've decided I want him, and I'll make sure I consume his every thought—during practice, in the locker room, even in his dreams.

I flash a mischievous grin, letting my gaze slowly rake over the new assistant coach from head to toe, lingering just a bit too long to be appropriate. "Oh, and welcome to the team . . . *Becks.*"

Beckett

CHAPTER THREE

The rich scent of coffee and fresh pastries greets me as I step into the cozy indie coffee shop. Places like this are becoming a welcome part of my new routine here in Rosewood Bay. Supporting local businesses feels good, and the quality far surpasses the big corporate chains.

I order my usual—large coffee, dark roast, with a shit ton of sugar. The corners of my mouth twitch upward in a fleeting smile.

The barista hands me my drink, and I take a sip, savoring the perfect balance of bitterness and sweetness, then I grab a handful of sugar packets and stuff them in my pocket for later. Never hurts to be prepared.

Stepping outside with my drink, I breathe in the refreshing sea breeze rolling in off the harbor. Rosewood Bay sprawls out before me like a freaking postcard—a little slice of the high life on the North Shore of Long Island. Mansions, country clubs, designer shops. It's like the Hamptons' flashy kid brother. Old money and new money, all rubbing elbows.

Quite the change of pace from my humble roots back in Tennessee. My shoebox apartment above the coffee shop seems comically out of place amid the opulence.

I let out a dry chuckle thinking about it. Even with the coaching job's housing stipend, the prices in this state are a real kick in the teeth. At least it's just me and my cat.

My jaw clenches.

Every apartment I checked out was non-pet friendly, and I wasn't giving my cat away. Not after what she's been through because of me. So I snuck her in and pray every day my landlord doesn't make an unexpected visit.

I cross the street toward the concrete path along the harbor. This move is supposed to be a fresh start. I wasn't sure how this coaching job would go. I'd been avoiding hockey ever since my NHL career ended so abruptly.

But I needed a change. I'd been spinning my wheels in that dead-end advertising job for too damn long.

My ex only made the decision easier. Never thought I'd be the type of person to slap a restraining order on someone.

But the ultimate deciding factor happened during my second interview when Coach Nieminen disclosed the disturbing details of how that reprehensible individual physically assaulted Jackson Reed.

I still feel sick thinking about what he endured.

However, there was something unsettling about the way Nieminen casually dismissed the former coach's abrupt departure. And Crestwood's president, Alfred Ghoram, made a point to emphasize the influential and powerful nature of many of the players' parents.

The message was received loud and clear.

My phone buzzes in my pocket, jolting me out of my thoughts. I fish it out, my brother's name flashing on the screen. I answer, then press the phone to my ear.

"Hey, B. How's it going?" Tommy asks.

"Oh, you know. Living the dream." My tone drips with sarcasm. "How's life across the pond?"

"Not bad. Still single, but what else is new?" He chuckles. "Just wanted to check in. I know being back in the hockey world can't be easy, not after everything that happened with your injury . . ."

I grimace, my free hand reflexively rubbing the spot on my lower back where the torn psoas muscle ended my playing career just as it was beginning. "Hanging in. Team's full of rich, entitled brats who're keeping me on my toes."

"Sounds like fun." He's silent for a moment. "Still don't agree with you not pressing charges against Noah. What if he doesn't stop? A restraining order's just a piece of paper, you know."

I sigh, scrubbing a hand over my face. "Made sure to cover my tracks when I left. He's got no idea where I am."

"Good. Just be careful, all right? I worry about you, big brother."

"I'll be fine."

The words are no sooner out when Viktor Novotny appears up ahead, lounging against his blue McLaren GT and throwing me a flirty little wave.

Right on cue, my walls slam up, my shoulders squaring. "Tommy, I gotta go. I'll call you later."

Before my brother can respond, I end the call, then slide the phone back into my pocket. I take another swig of my coffee before tossing it into a nearby trash can as I approach the insolent brat who I strongly suspect has been stalking me.

He's made a few out of the blue appearances. On campus, it might be understandable, and while Rosewood Bay is a small, incorporated village, the frequency of our encounters is a bit too convenient to be random—he's definitely following me.

Time to set some boundaries, something I should've done at the gala when Nieminen pointed out who he was.

I took notice when he first approached me at the bar. And his reaction when our eyes met—the way he called me pretty—fuck, I probably would've taken him home.

And he's definitely my type.

Bratty.

Then he just had to open that entitled mouth of his. Yeah, I stuck out like a sore thumb amongst the elite. But fuck, I didn't need to be insulted. And the stunt he pulled in the bathroom—talk about a walking red flag.

None of that matters because at the end of the day he's my player, and no way am I crossing *that* line.

"The fuck are you doing here, Novotny?"

He flashes me that infuriating, self-assured grin that makes me want to wipe it off his face. "Just admiring the scenery, Becks."

His eyes shamelessly roam over my body in a manner that's far too intimate. The audacious brat has pulled the same stunt during practices, even after I've corrected him.

I snarl, my patience wearing thin. "Cut the crap. I'm your coach, not your buddy or whatever twisted shit you're imagining."

A gentle breeze off the harbor carries the scent of his cologne toward me—a blend of bergamot, rosemary, and a hint of citrus—and despite my best efforts to resist, I find myself inhaling deeply.

Fuck, he smells good.

Viktor's pale blue eyes, the ones that resemble a sheet of ice in the rink, are almost translucent in the sunlight as he takes a step closer, getting all up in my personal space with that bratty attitude cranked up to eleven. "Where's the fun in that, Becks?"

Without thinking, my hand shoots out, grabbing him by the chin. Hard. The smirk slides right off his face, and his eyes go wide as I force him to meet my steely gaze. His body slackens instantly, and a blush creeps up his neck as his pupils dilate.

No. No. No.

Fuck!

He can't respond like that. Not to me. But as my grip tightens on his chin, a deep primal part doesn't want him to respond to anyone else like that either.

I take a slow breath, then release it, fighting off the growing lust.

Boundaries.

I need to establish boundaries.

"Listen up, you cocky little shit. You *will* address me as Coach or Coach Harper. Nothing else. Got it?" My voice is a deep rumble, laced with authority.

Viktor nods frantically, squirming a bit as his lips part a touch.

"Answer me, Novotny."

"Yes, Sir . . . I mean, Coach."

I release him, taking a step back. My heart's pounding in my chest, my cock's starting to wake up, and my blood thrums with a mix of annoyance and something I don't want to name. "Good. Now, keep it professional. No more showing up out of the blue, no more pushing my buttons. We clear?"

"Yes, Coach Harper," he says, but there's a defiant glint in his eye that tells me this is far from over.

I nod, then turn to walk away. If I stay this close to him any longer, I may do something I regret.

This move's already promising to be a challenge. But I'm here to do a job, to start fresh and leave my baggage behind. And I won't let anyone, least of all some cocky, privileged hockey player, disrupt that.

Especially one who I'm coaching. One who's strictly off-limits.

Viktor

CHAPTER FOUR

I'm on fire today, blocking every shot that comes my way like a goddamn ninja. Glove save, stick save, pad save—you name it, I'm doing it. It's like the hockey gods are smiling down on me, blessing me with superhuman reflexes and an unbeatable swagger, even if it's just a practice scrimmage.

"All right, boys, run it again." Coach Nieminen's voice booms across the ice.

I smirk behind my mask as I make another incredible save. But let's be real, I'm not just putting on this show for the love of hockey. No, I've got an ulterior motive.

"Hey, Becks!" I call out, unable to stop myself. "Did you see that last save? Pretty impressive, right?"

So what if I got all subby and shit the other day? And there's no denying the way his pupils dilated too.

Can't school every feature, not against me. Not when I'm looking dead into those two different colored irises.

Fuck.

I need to stop thinking about that. Wearing a cup and getting hard is the most uncomfortable shit ever.

"Focus on the drill, Novotny," my stupid goalie coach yells.

Okay, he's not stupid. Sure, I've got natural talent, but Rinne's made me better. And we're continuing to work on that dumb habit I have of overcommitting to the right.

But Beckett-fucking-Harper's a damn brick wall. He barely glances my way. It's like I'm invisible, just another cog in the machine.

And it's starting to piss me off.

I mean, come on. I'm Viktor Novotny. Goalies like me don't grow on trees. I'm a once-in-a-generation talent, a force to be reckoned with. Would it kill him to throw a little attention my way? A nod of approval? A 'Nice save, Novotny'?

Hell, I'd settle for a grunt of acknowledgement at this point.

But no. He's too busy focusing on the other players, especially the rookies.

What do I have to do to get his attention? Strip naked and do a fucking dance at center ice?

Actually . . .

"Novotny!" Coach Nieminen's voice snaps me out of my thoughts. "Pay attention. We've got a big match coming up and I need you sharp."

I toss the puck I'm holding, then kick it like it's a soccer ball. Since when have I become easy to ignore?

As the scrimmage continues, I put in all my effort as if it was a real game, showcasing my work ethic. Maybe that will get my new assistant coach's attention. I continue defending my crease, each save more impressive than the last, each one a silent plea for Beckett to just fucking notice me.

But he's focusing on the rookie who's taken over Alexei's spot, his mouth moving as he gives him pointers and advice.

I bang my stick against the ice and snarl.

Eventually, practice ends, and by the time we hit the showers, my mood has me feeling like a wilted lettuce leaf in a forgotten corner of the fridge, slowly turning into a slimy, unappetizing blob of sadness and despair.

"What the fuck are you moping about again. Seriously, you're making me want to call Eli." Jackson eyes me as I drop onto the bench after my shower.

Already in my boxers—always put them on in the shower so no one sees the scars all over my ass— I sulk my way through getting dressed, only half-listening to the locker room chatter around me.

Zach pulls his sweatshirt on, then quirks a brow at me. "Take it your latest obsession is still ignoring you."

I shoot him the finger. "He's just playing hard to get. He'll fall in love with me sooner or later."

Connor eyes me, brow quirked. "Ever consider you're barking up the wrong tree? You know . . . that he might be straight."

Jackson snickers and I roll my eyes. "Not sure what he is, but the whole interaction at the harbor did confirm one thing—he's attracted to me. And that's all that matters."

He bumps me with his shoulder. "We still on for that movie with Eli later?"

"You would know if you belonged to our group chat. Can't believe you assholes are vers."

He whacks me in the chest. "Told you to just add us both."

I palm his face and push him away. "Not how it works. Only one person per couple, and neither of you want to choose. Bunch of losers."

Jackson groans and turns to finish getting dressed as the locker room empties out, leaving just the two of us because he's taking his sweet time, as usual, fiddling with his hair in the mirror like he's about to walk a fucking runway instead of return to our dorm room.

Just as I'm about to tell him to hurry the fuck up, Beckett walks by. Jackson stiffens, his hand frozen mid-primp, and I instinctively walk to him, placing myself between him and Beckett.

I know my friend's still fucked up over what happened last year, no matter how much he tries to play it off. That piece of shit did a number on him, and it kills me that I wasn't there to stop it.

Never again, though.

Not when I've got eyes on him 24/7. And by "eyes," I mean, the tracker I implanted between his neck and shoulder. He's been impossible to tag. But then the fucker asked me to come by one day to freeze a bunch of paintballs—God knows why—and he eventually passed out from pain meds.

It's just . . . a precaution. The safety of those I care about is an obsession of mine, one that can't be helped, especially not after what happened with my twin sister.

Turns out, getting kidnapped comes with the territory of the family business. But it fucked me up not knowing where she was, if she was okay.

Luckily, my parents tagged us when we were infants. Seems I'm not weird, it's just a common practice in our family.

Even Alexei tagged Eli. He slipped a tracker into him when they first got together. He thinks I don't know about it but please. I've got the info too. Just in case.

Connor was the easiest to tag. And my aunt gave me Alexei's info, same way he has mine.

Zach, on the other hand, was a bit of a challenge. He'll kill me if he knew I'd tagged him after our little play session. But what Zach doesn't know won't hurt him.

Or me.

Hopefully.

Beckett's gaze lands on me, then softens, and I feel a flicker of . . . something. Respect, maybe? Appreciation? I'm not sure, but I kind of like it.

"Good practice today, you two," he says, then continues on his way, and I let out a deep breath. But he suddenly stops, then bends to pick something off the floor. "What—"

My lucky card.

I lunge forward and snatch the burnt Ace of Spades from his hand, our fingers briefly touching, sending electrical bolts shooting across my skin. "It's mine."

He looks down at the card and smirks. All hockey players are superstitious, and some of us have good luck charms.

Jackson sags forward when Beckett leaves, his hands resting on the countertop, his cocky facade slipping for just a moment.

"You okay?" I keep my voice low as I tuck the card into my wallet.

He nods, not quite meeting my eyes. "Yeah, yeah. I'm fine. Just . . . You know."

"Let's get out of here."

We collect our shit and walk out of the rink together, but then go our separate ways. He heads to our room over in Young Hall and I make my way to the back lot where my ugly black minivan is parked to start my nightly routine and then pick up some ice cream.

No one knows about this car. It's my little secret, my escape when I need to get away from the pressure of being Viktor Novotny, hockey *and* chemistry prodigy, and resident troublemaker.

Okay, that's bullshit.

The minivan is my stalkermobile, the one no one would ever suspect I drive. The Chrysler Pacifica also blends into Rosewood Bay, a favorite amongst the nannies and au pairs. But it's common enough that it doesn't stand out on those occasions outside of our incorporated village either.

And it has ample enough room for when we need to transport a body or two. Like Coach Buckland's.

I slide into the driver's seat, turn the key in the ignition, then pull out of the lot, heading in the direction of Beckett's apartment.

Not sure if he thought I'd head home after our little encounter at the harbor a few days ago. But if I'm anything, it's patient. Well, mostly patient. And he wasn't very stealthy, only waited twenty minutes before heading back home.

Turns out he lives in one of the apartments above the coffee shop and, fortunately for me, not one that faces the water.

The drive is relatively short. Who wants to live far from work anyway? I park a few streets over from Beckett's place, not wanting to risk being caught if my coach happens to look out the window.

After grabbing my psycho nun mask and binoculars, I hop out of the minivan, and make my way toward the building across from Beckett's. It's the perfect vantage point.

I slip around to the back toward the rusty old fire escape, then take the stairs two at a time, my heart pounding with a heady mixture of adrenaline and anticipation. There's just something about the rush of doing something I know I shouldn't. It's like a drug, and I'm a hopeless addict.

Once my mask is in place, I pull the hood of my sweatshirt up, blending into the darkness as I creep to the edge of the roof, my eyes already scanning the windows of the building across the street.

This isn't my first rodeo. I've done this little song and dance about three times already. It's how I know Beckett

Harper spends most of his time reading or playing sudoku before bed. And that he never goes out.

Boring.

But he hasn't brought anyone home either, and I haven't noticed anyone else living there. So, that's a plus.

I zero in on his window. At least he has the lights on today with the blinds up. Right after I take a seat on the parapet, Beckett comes into view, a towel wrapped around his waist. Stray droplets glisten on his skin, tracing tantalizing paths down the planes of his chest and abs. His thick, dark brown hair is tousled and damp.

He walks over to the dresser, his back to the window, and I lean forward, trying to get a better look. The broad expanse of his shoulders tapers to a trim waist, all lean muscle and taut skin. But there, peeking out from under the towel near his hip . . .

A scar.

Jagged and silvery, standing out starkly against his tanned skin. It appears old, long-healed, but no less startling.

A sports injury, maybe? But before I can ponder further, Beckett turns. And holy hell . . .

I haven't seen him naked yet. Well, not in real life, just my fantasies. But even my wild imagination didn't do justice to the sheer magnitude of what he's packing.

The towel does absolutely nothing to hide the massive erection jutting out from his hips, obscenely tenting the fabric. I catch myself licking my lips, transfixed by the thought of that beast splitting me open, ruining me for anyone else.

He moves to the bed, and I swallow hard as he undoes the towel, letting it drop to the floor, revealing his gloriously naked body. And when I say glorious, I mean it. The man is a goddamn Adonis, all hard planes and rippling muscles.

But instead of putting on his boxer briefs, he just tosses them aside and sits on the edge of the mattress, his dick standing at attention. For a moment, he just stares at it, like he's fighting some internal battle. His hands clench into fists, and I hold my breath, waiting to see what he'll do.

My jaw drops and I lean forward a bit too much, catching myself before I fall right off the edge when he starts to stroke himself, just lazy strokes up and down his shaft.

And when he starts to tease the head, rubbing his thumb over the slit, I'm done for. He's taking his time, savoring every moment, and I can't look away. It's like watching a work of art unfold before my very eyes.

Soon enough, he's picking up the pace, fist flying over his shaft. He leans back, bracing himself with one hand on the bed, hips lifting to meet his strokes. His head tips back, exposing the long column of his throat.

God, what I wouldn't give to be in that room with him. To be on my knees, choking on that gorgeous dick. I'd let him do anything he wanted to me, let him use me however he saw fit.

I grab my own length that's already punching at my zipper, wanting to break free. I'm hard as a fucking rock, leaking in my boxers like a goddamn teenager.

Sweat glistens on his skin, a flush spreading down his chest, and then his back arches off the bed as he comes, painting his stomach and chest with ropes of white.

My desperate moan cuts through the night as I come in my jeans. But I can't even be embarrassed about it. Not when Beckett suddenly sits up, grabbing his cell phone from the nightstand, his face twisting into pure rage.

He doesn't just toss the phone aside. He flings it across the room. It hits the wall and falls to the floor as he stands up, pacing the room like a caged animal before disappearing from view.

On the floor, the device continues to light up like a damn Christmas tree.

Who the fuck is blowing up his phone like that? But whoever they are, they better back the fuck off.

Because Beckett Harper is mine.

Even if he still doesn't know it . . . yet.

Beckett

CHAPTER FIVE

Two days. It's been two goddamn days since that night, and I still can't get it out of my head.

I shouldn't have let my mind wander to Novotny while I jacked off. He's my player, for Christ's sake.

Off limits.

I shake my head, disgusted. I'm supposed to be the responsible one here. The adult. I can't have these kinds of thoughts about him. Even if he does go out of his way to get my attention as if he craves it.

And yeah, no matter how much I try to keep my distance, there's no denying he commands attention when he's on the ice because he's good.

Really good.

I'm not sure why he hasn't signed with the Islanders yet. Well, outside of the fact he needs to mature. Though, he wouldn't be the first NHL player needing to grow the fuck up.

But there's something more to Novotny, as if he can't help himself. I just can't put my finger on it.

He's got this raw, unbridled energy that's both captivating and concerning. It's like he's constantly teetering on the edge of control and chaos, and part of me wants to be the one to rein him in.

Fuck. I can't think like that. It's inappropriate, unprofessional.

I run a hand over my face, feeling the scratch of stubble, then turn my attention back to the team and pace along the sidelines of the gym, my arms crossed tightly over my chest.

As they go through their off-ice training, I reflect on how things are going so far in my new role. Being back in the hockey world, even from the coaching side, has been both invigorating and challenging.

I'm finding I enjoy it more than I anticipated. Working with the team, helping them hone their skills and strategies, is surprisingly fulfilling. Even with the occasional headaches—aka Novotny—I feel like I'm settling into a good rhythm here.

Speaking of the bratty goalie, he's spotting Reed on the bench press. There's a seriousness to him, a protectiveness in the way he hovers over his friend. Like a few days ago in the locker room when Reed had tensed up. Novotny instantly moved closer, putting himself between us like a shield.

What else don't I know about him? What other depths are hidden beneath that flashy, flirtatious exterior?

My phone starts buzzing again.

I thought I was done with Noah, but changing my number didn't help because my ex is apparently more resourceful than I gave him credit for.

I delete his texts without reading them, just like I did last time. And the time before that. It's the only way I know how to cope.

"Hey, Becks, what's got you grumpier than normal?"

I grind my molars, not in the mood for Novotny's brattiness. "Are we going to continue to have this problem? Do I need to go to admin because you keep disrespecting me?"

Reed whistles, egging on his friend, but I just cross my arms and stare down the Titans' goalie.

Novotny just walks to the leg press as if my threat means absolutely nothing to him.

I turn back to the rest of the team and pace the length of the gym as they work through their drills. "Pick up the pace, gentlemen! Every single one of you needs to be in peak condition this season."

Knight and Walsh are locked into their workouts, Reed half-focuses between his and keeping an eye on me. I make sure to respect the large bubble of personal space he needs.

"Zach, watch your squats. You're leaning forward too much. Knees are crossing over your toes."

The look he shoots me makes my skin crawl. Or I should say the void in his eyes. Then he just turns away, dismissing me.

Nieminen called him the resident psychopath.

Can't say I fully agree. Sometimes he appears robotic, cold even, but other times, I catch a brief glimpse of something else. Regardless, there are times—like now—when he's putting off that "steer clear" energy.

"We done yet?" Novotny places his hands on his hips and juts his chin toward the clock on the wall. "Some of us have things to do. You know, lives that don't involve Soduko."

My spine straightens and eyes narrow. "You've got thirty more minutes left."

He just rolls his eyes, that infuriating little smirk still playing at the corners of his mouth as he reaches for a set of free weights, his well-defined muscles flexing as he starts in on a set of bicep curls.

I let my gaze linger for a moment too long on his impressive upper body—the way his shirt stretches taut across his broad chest, the veins tracing along his forearms, the tantalizing curve of his perky ass . . .

"See something you like, *Coach*?" He's watching me in the mirror, one eyebrow arched, a knowing little smirk on that irritatingly handsome face.

Fuck.

I set my jaw and turn away, barking out orders to the rest of the team, determined to pretend that charged little moment never happened. And luckily, the brat keeps to himself for the rest of the session.

After dismissing the team, I walk to my office and flop into the chair. But the moment I catch my breath, the blond chaos demon with those ice blue eyes enters the office, a full-on devilish smirk plastered on his face. He walks in like he owns the place, sitting on the edge of my desk, invading my personal space.

I lean back in the chair. "What can I help you with?"

"Oh, come on now, Becks. You know what I want. Just like I now know what you want."

"Watch yourself, brat." My voice comes out as a deep rumble, a tone he responded to last time.

A blush starts to creep up his neck, but still, he quirks a brow, challenging me. "What are you going to do about it, *Coach*? You going to put me in my place?"

I stand, then get in his face, placing my arms on either side of him, bracketing him in. "Be careful what you wish for Viktor. You might just get it."

"Promise?"

"You can't handle me."

He leans in closer, his lips brushing against the shell of my ear. "Bet I can."

He's goading me, and I need to back away, but a mixture of frustration and arousal is lighting up my veins, and if I don't do something, I'll combust.

Quickly walking to the door, I slam it shut and lock it, then turn back to him. "On your knees and crawl to me. Now."

He hesitates for a minute, then drops and crawls over like a fucking cat. And when I say cat, I mean, with that mischievous expression plastered on his face. Oh, he's dead wrong if he thinks he has the upper hand.

Novotny comes to a stop right in front of me, sits back on his heels and looks up, his blue eyes meeting mine through thick lashes.

I reach down and fist his wavy blond hair as I pull my cock out with my other hand, then slap him across the face with it. "Didn't know you were such a slut."

Instead of answering, his tongue lashes out and swipes along my cock. My fingers tighten in his hair as I shove myself into his mouth, pushing deep until he gags. My pulse races at the sound and I start fucking his mouth until he's drooling. "Still think you can handle me, Chaos?"

When his hands start to slide up my thighs, I push all the way in until I bottom out, then hold him there with both of my hands around the back of his head. His throat tightens around me and my balls pull tight.

But I stave off my orgasm. I'm not done teaching the brat a lesson.

I yank him off when he starts slapping my legs, but not right away, then chuckle. "What's the matter? Didn't you say you could handle me?"

He gasps for air, his chin covered in saliva, cheeks streaked with tears. "Y-yes . . ." His voice is raspy.

I push back into his mouth, and fuck it roughly, my balls smacking against his chin. Using his hair for leverage, I continue to drive into him, my grunts mixing with his sloppy, wet gagging. My orgasm is close, my body tensing, and I pull out, not wanting to come down his throat.

He hasn't earned that.

"You need to cut the shit. I'm tired of the disrespect." I start pumping myself and when he leans in, I yank him back with the hand still fisting his hair. "Don't take what's not given."

After a few more strokes, the tension in my body snaps and my release hits hard. When I'm done and the post-orgasm bliss starts to fade, I push him away and he tumbles back onto his ass. His eyes are wide and mouth agape, his face covered in my cum.

His tongue flicks across his upper lip, tasting it.

Tasting me.

My breath catches in my throat, a shiver running down my spine.

Fuck, I need to get out of here before things spiral further out of control.

"Clean yourself up and go home, Viktor."

I pull my shorts back up, head to my desk and grab my keys and wallet, not waiting for him to respond. I walk right past him, each step echoing my racing heart, and bolt out the door.

What the fuck did I just do?

Viktor

CHAPTER SIX

The moment my skates hit the ice, the roar of the crowd crashes over me like a tidal wave. It's electric, intoxicating—the first official game of the season, and it's all eyes on us.

On me.

Quinnipiac's got some new rookie they think is hot shit.

Please.

I've seen the kid play. He's fast, but he's gonna learn quickly that speed won't save him from getting crushed out here. Welcome to hell, fresh meat.

But as I skate to the net, everything's different. It's our first game without Alexei. My eyes drift to the seats right behind me and, sure enough, my BFF is right there with his two friends.

Eli's waving with a stupid grin on his face, wearing his custom sweatshirt with Alexei's number on it.

What a dork.

I smile and wave back, then tap my helmet, feeling the familiar crinkle of the burnt Ace of Spades card tucked inside. My lucky charm. A reminder of the time Alexei and I got shitfaced on some vodka and nearly set ourselves on fire while playing poker.

Mom almost murdered me, but it was so worth it. Played a game the next day with that charred card in my helmet and got my first fucking shutout. Been playing with it in my helmet ever since.

After stretching, I go about tearing up the ice in the crease, but I can't help sneaking a peek at the bench. *Coach Harper*, that fucker. He's been ignoring me since that shit in his office, when he had me on my knees, choking on his dick.

The way he just used me, dominated me . . . Fuck, it was hot. The man is definitely into men. Didn't even bat an eye about shoving his dick into my mouth.

And he called me Chaos. A nickname. My stomach flutters at the memory.

Thought I was finally winning him over, but then he just walked away like it was nothing.

Fucking typical.

I'm used to being the center of attention. I crave it, need it like I need fucking air. But I'm also used to being left behind. Rejected. Abandoned. I'm always too much, too crazy, too intense for anyone to handle. Story of my goddamn life.

And Beckett?

He's just the latest asshole to make me feel that way.

Jackson skates over and taps my pads with his stick. "What's got your panties in a bunch?"

"Fuck off."

He straightens up, brows pinched and lips pressed into a tight line. "Uh, Novy, you okay?"

Connor and Zach skate over, and Connor looks at Jackson. "What's going on?"

"He's . . . gloomy."

The three stare at me and I do some side-to-sides, warming up my legs and ignoring them. While I normally share my sexual escapades the way people talk about the weather, this time I don't.

And I'm not sure why. They already know I have a thing for our new coach. Maybe it's because, for once, someone managed to outplay me at my own game. It's both infuriating and intoxicating.

Especially after tasting him, feeling his hands in my hair, his dick down my throat. Fuck, just thinking about it makes me hard.

I want more.

Need more.

Coach Nieminen calls us in for the pep talk, saving me from the impending interrogation. We skate to the bench, but I hang at the back, only half-listening, my eyes glued to our assistant coach. Fucker won't even look at me.

But that's okay. I like a challenge.

Jackson throws an arm around me, knocking his helmet against mine. "Ready to fuck shit up?"

"Always."

As both teams line up, I go through my ritual. Tap the posts, tap my helmet, and feel that lucky card rubbing against my hair. Me and that card, we're the MVPs of our games. The most valuable and most powerful.

The puck drops and it's on. I'm in the fucking zone, blocking shot after shot like a goddamn wall. Not like I have a choice with the rookie who replaced Alexei shitting the bed out there. Zach's ready to murder the kid.

"Henneman, get your fucking head out of your ass," I yell as he skates off to the bench.

Connor and Jackson score, putting us up two points by the end of the first. Connor skates to me as we head off the ice. "Still don't get why you didn't just sign with the Islanders."

I snort. "And miss out on all this? No fucking way."

But honestly, I've been thinking about it more and more, especially since Alexei went pro. The Islanders drafted me, wanted me. But I wanted to study science.

People always assume I'm dumb, but they couldn't be more wrong. I'm a fucking Chemical and Molecular Engineering major, top of my class.

It's my other obsession.

But I can't call it love, though. No, my drive comes purely from hating Big Pharma. So, I turned down the contract the Islanders offered and came to Crestwood.

Zach joins us. "Going to plaster Henneman into the boards myself if he doesn't get his shit together."

Second period's a little better. Zach makes good on his threat, slamming our rookie defenseman into the boards after the dumbass screens me, causing the puck to slip through five-hole.

Third period is fierce, especially since we're only up by one. Coach Nieminen benches Henneman. His replacement doesn't play well with Zach, but at least the kid has skill. Quinnipiac gets a breakaway, and the player tries to deke but I poke the puck away.

It's a fucking madhouse in front of the net. I'm doing splits, reaching, bending in ways I didn't know I could. Another shot. This time, the puck hits my glove and I smother it against my chest.

The horn sounds. Game over. We won.

I grab the puck and toss it over the glass to Eli before hitting the handshake line. The dork's grinning so wide, I swear his face is gonna split. Bet he'll lose his shit the first time Alexei tosses him a puck.

After shaking hands with the other teams' coaches, I make my way off the ice. But when I skate past Coach Harper, he has the audacity to look at me with a proud fucking smile. Like he thinks we're cool now.

Please.

I blow right past him, ignoring his outstretched hand. I feel his eyes on my back, but I don't give him the satisfaction of turning around because Viktor Novotny doesn't get outplayed.

Beckett Harper wants to play games?

Fine.

I'll show him just how petty and bratty and fucking entitled I can be.

Beckett

CHAPTER SEVEN

The pub's dimly lit, the low murmur of conversation and the clink of glasses filling the air. It's been a while since I've been out like this, just grabbing drinks with a friend. But Rinne insisted, said I needed to get out of my apartment and socialize like a normal human being.

He's not wrong. I've been holed up in my place since I moved to Rosewood Bay a few weeks ago. I just wanted to take the time to enjoy the peace and focus on coaching. The only person I bother talking to on occasion is my brother.

"So, how're you finding it? Coaching the team?" Rinne asks, taking a sip of his beer, his eyes fixed on me.

I lean back in my chair, considering the question. "It's different. Good different, mostly. The guys are talented, driven. A handful sometimes."

Rinne chuckles, nodding. "Things have changed since I was drafted. Seems like more and more kids wanna go to college first. At least more than there used to be. Like

Novotny. Kid's a fucking wall in the net. But hell . . . you see his grades?"

I tense at the mention of Viktor, images of him on his knees, my cock in his mouth, flashing through my mind. I take a long pull of my beer, trying to drown the memories. "No. They bad?"

"Quite the opposite. The annoying shit's like a genius. Been on the Dean's list every semester. Chemical and Molecular Engineering major, no less."

"Fuck." I hate how surprised I am to hear that, like because of his behavior, I figured he wasn't smart. "Still, Novotny needs to get his behavior in check."

"Those four are something else. Just count your blessings Petrov isn't here anymore. And that Reed's calmed down."

I quirk a brow, resting my elbows on the table as I lean forward. "They're that bad? I mean, Nieminen told me to steer clear of their shit."

Rinne whistles. "They've all got lawyers on speed dial, and their families have deeper pockets than anyone I know, including team owners. But Reed's dating Killian Blackwell so a lot of the shit with the Serpents seems to have cooled off."

Killian Blackwell was one of the top picks in the draft a few years ago. Phenomenal player.

After finishing off my beer, I pick at the rest of my fries and turn the conversation away from work. "Remember that game against the Bruins in your third year? You made that ridiculous glove save in overtime. Thought the crowd was going to riot."

Rinne laughs, his eyes lighting up. "Oh, man. I thought Lucic was going to murder me. The look on his face . . ."

"You were with Tampa Bay, right? Before the injury?" Rinne asks, his tone cautious.

I grimace and stare out the window, focusing on a minivan across the street as the memory of that moment, the searing pain as my psoas muscle tore, flashes through my mind. "Yeah. One season. Made it to round three of the playoffs before I tore my psoas. Ended my career just like that."

"Shit, man. That's rough," Rinne says, genuine sympathy in his eyes. "Psoas injuries are no joke. Had a teammate go through that once. Took him months to recover."

I nod, taking another sip of my beer. "Yeah, the surgery and rehab were a bitch. Thought I was going to lose my mind being cooped up like that. But it is what it is. Took me a while to come to terms with it. Got pretty low for a bit, took a job I hated just to pay the bills. But I'm glad to be back in hockey, even if it's not the way I planned."

He shakes his head, then flings a fry at me. "Your rookie ass snowed me one game."

"Only because your dumbass kept whacking me in the back of the calves." I laugh, remembering that game. Man, I really miss playing.

"Gotta defend my crease, numbnuts."

We trade stories back and forth, reminiscing about our playing days. It's nice having someone who understands, who's been through the same things. Rinne's easy to talk to, his laid-back demeanor putting me at ease.

"All right, gotta ask . . . What's your thing?"

His brows furrow, then lift as he chuckles. "You mean my superstition? Nothing too crazy. I'd wear the same socks—they had bacon designs on them—every game. But wouldn't wash them if we were on a winning streak."

"You fucking serious?" I shake my head, laughing so hard I snort. "Where'd you keep those nasty things between games?"

"In a plastic baggy. Goalies, man. We're a different breed." Rinne leans back and crosses his arms in front of his chest. "So, asshole. What was yours?"

"Used to eat a box of Lucky Charms but would pick out all the cereal and just eat the marshmallows."

Rinne laughs, then regales me with tales of his latest fishing trips. He invites me to join him sometime, says he knows a great spot not too far from here.

"Might just take you up on that," I say, surprised to find that I actually mean it.

It's been a long time since I had a friend, someone to just shoot the shit with. It feels good, normal in a way that my life hasn't been in a long time.

We finish our food and settle the bill, Rinne insisting on paying. "My treat, Beckett. Consider it a welcome to Rosewood Bay gift."

I shake my head but smile. "All right, but next time it's on me."

"Deal."

Rinne walks to his car, and I head to my R1. The sleek lines of the motorcycle gleam under the streetlights, and I feel a thrill of anticipation as I swing my leg over the seat. After putting on my helmet, I turn the key and the familiar roar of the engine comes to life beneath me.

This, right here, is my freedom. The open road, the vibrations of the bike thrumming through my body. It's the only thing that clears my head, makes me feel like I can breathe again.

I take the long way home, savoring the winding roads, the cool night air. By the time I'm back in Rosewood Bay, I'm even more settled, more like myself.

Turning down the street toward my apartment, I pass a minivan that looks just like the one that was parked outside the pub. But it's a common model.

If ever the world created an ugly model of car it would have to be the minivan. They give me the ick.

After parking my bike in the lot behind the building, I head upstairs and unlock the door. The moment I flick on the light, a flash of white catches my eye as it makes its way under the couch.

She's hiding again. From me. I hate this.

Figured by now, she'd settle in. I miss my sweet girl. Miss her cuddling up to me as I read before bed.

Fucking Noah.

Raking my hands through my hair, I head to the window to pull the blinds down for the night. But as I reach for the cord, I freeze. Someone's on the roof of the building across the street. And they're staring directly at me.

Or at least I think they are.

Can't tell exactly with the mask they're wearing—a crystalline mask, decorated like a demonic nun with black, soulless eyes that seem to bore into me.

Fear lances through me, cold and sharp, when the person waves at me, each finger curling slowly.

He found me.

But the fear is quickly overtaken by a deep, burning rage. I close the blinds with a sharp yank, turn off the lights, and stride out of my apartment, slamming the door behind me.

One way or another, this ends tonight.

Viktor

CHAPTER EIGHT

The corner of my mouth tugs into a smirk. Yeah, I wanted Becks to see me, especially after I had to sit and watch him and Rinne getting all cozy together. They looked so comfortable, leaning in close to talk. Then Becks started laughing. And smiling.

My skin heats, jaw clenching.

I know Coach Rinne's happily married, but seeing them together, all buddy-buddy, it just rubbed me the wrong way.

I barely kept my ass in the minivan, fighting off the urge to march over and stake my claim. To sit in Beckett's lap and show Rinne exactly who he belongs to.

Beckett is mine. Mine to want, mine to obsess over. And I don't share.

So, I figured I'd let my grumpy coach catch me watching him. Not surprised he closed the shades. He's probably freaked out. What I don't understand is why he shut the lights.

Either way, doubt I'll be seeing anything for the rest of the night. Might as well go home and come up with a new game plan to win him over.

I walk back to the fire escape, the cool night air whipping around me, my mask firmly in place. From far away, everyone thinks this thing is made of crystals, and it was when I first purchased it. But then I had them replaced with diamonds. Because I can.

Had the base waterproofed first. Glad I did with how many times I've had to wash blood off it.

My feet barely hit the pavement after I get to the bottom of the fire escape when the back of my hoodie is yanked and I'm slammed into the opposite wall face first, a large body pinning me.

"What the fuck are you doing here, Noah?" Beckett's voice is low, dangerous, his hot breath skating over my ear.

Noah?

Who the fuck is Noah?

But before I can get a word out, Beckett spins me around, shoving my back into the wall. My head bounces off the brick, hard enough to make me grimace.

His hand wraps around my throat and squeezes, causing my breath to hitch.

A thrill runs through me at the contact, at the feeling of his body pressed against mine. This is what I've been craving, what I've been dreaming about since that night in his office.

He's seething, his face inches from mine, but I'm not afraid. If anything, I'm intrigued. Is this Noah guy the one who's been blowing up Beckett's phone?

"How'd you find me?" He snarls, pressing his forearm against my chest, pinning me in place.

He reaches up with his free hand, ripping the mask off. The cool air feels good against my flushed skin, and I can't help but smirk. "Evening, Becks."

"Novotny?" He blinks a few times, features scrunching as his grip on my throat loosens slightly. "What the hell are you doing here?"

"Isn't it obvious?" I lean forward, brushing my lips against his, just a teasing taste.

He growls, tightening his fingers around my throat, cutting off my air. "You need to learn to respect boundaries. This shit isn't okay."

Even as spots dance in my vision, I can't help but laugh and push into his grasp, winking at him. "Oh, come on now. We both know you want me."

"You don't know what you're talking about."

"So, you just enjoy using my throat, then tossing me aside like garbage after you blow your load?"

"What?" Beckett's eyes widen, and he abruptly lets go of my throat and steps back. "That's . . . that's . . . You're not garbage."

"Oh, so is it because of Noah, then?"

"You have no idea what you're talking about." He runs a hand through his hair, tugging at the roots as he paces. "I left because I fucked up. I'm your coach, Viktor. I crossed the line. You're off-limits."

I roll my eyes, waving a dismissive hand. "Oh, please. Don't give me the power dynamic speech."

"It's not a speech, it's—"

I cut him off, not wanting to hear it. "None of the staff at Crestwood really have any power, Becks. The power belongs to the families of the students. Well, except for the scholarship students, of course."

Beckett's jaw clenches. "Doesn't matter. We can't do this."

"Be honest with me. If I'd signed with the Islanders rights after the draft, and you ran into me at a bar, would you have fucked me?"

His jaw ticks.

"Well, would you have?"

"Yeah." He shakes his head. "But that's not reality, so nothing can happen between us again."

I start trailing my hand down his chest, over his abs, feeling the heat of his skin through his shirt. "That ship sailed the moment you had me on my knees, *Coach*. The moment you fucked my face."

He grabs my wrist, stopping my exploration. His eyes are dark, dominating. "Remember what I said, Chaos. Don't take what's not given."

There it is again. That nickname. Does he even realize he's saying it? It makes me feel all fluttery inside, like I'm special.

I push the envelope, pressing my body against his once more, feeling the hard ridge of his erection against my hip. "But you want to give it to me, don't you, *Coach*? You want to lose control again."

Beckett's hand comes up, smacking my cheek. It's not hard enough to really sting, but it makes me whimper and my hips buck, my throbbing dick brushing against his muscular thigh.

He hisses through his teeth, stepping forward and pinning me between his chest and the brick wall.

"Are you going to punish me, Becks?" I ask, my voice breathy, needy.

He doesn't answer, just guides me to keep dry humping his thigh, harder and faster. I grip his arms, riding him shamelessly. "Beckett . . . Ohhhh, fuck."

I'm panting and whimpering, my body desperate and strung out, the friction driving me out of my mind. Everything coils up and I'm right there, right on the edge.

Beckett's mouth lowers to the shell of my ear. "Go home, Viktor. And knock off the stalking shit."

He steps back, putting distance between us, then walks away.

He can't leave. Not again.

"Wait!" I call out, hating how desperate I sound. "Becks, please."

But he doesn't turn around. Doesn't even pause. He just keeps walking, leaving me alone, frustrated and aching.

I lean my head back against the wall, closing my eyes and trying to catch my breath.

I don't get it. I'm offering myself to him on a fucking platter. Why won't he just take what he wants?

Because of this Noah guy? Because of some bullshit idea about power dynamics?

Or because . . . he doesn't want me?

"Chaos, get the fuck over here. Now."

My eyes open and I whip my head around. Beckett's standing at the curb, arms crossed. I pick my mask up off the floor, then jog to him.

"Since you want to push boundaries and continue to disobey me, your hands stay off your fucking cock."

My brows lift, mouth gaping. "What?"

His features tighten. "You heard me. No fucking coming."

A shiver runs down my spine, excitement mixing with the ache of denial. "For how long?"

He steps closer, gripping my chin and forcing me to look him in the eyes. "Until I say so, brat. And if you disobey me, if you even think about touching this . . ." His other hand ghosts over my dick, barely a whisper of touch, but it makes me whimper. "I'll know. And the consequences will be severe. Understand?"

I nod, my mouth dry, my heart pounding. "Yes, Coach."

"Good boy."

He releases me, then crosses the street back to his building. A grin spreads across my face, a giddy, reckless sort of joy bubbling up in my chest as I practically skip toward my stalkermobile to head home.

I'll take this as a win even though I would've rather him fuck me senseless.

Beckett

The chill of the rink seeps through my wool peacoat as I step out of the locker room and make my way to the bench, hands shoved deep in my pockets, I nod at Rinne as I take my place beside him. The tension in the air is palpable, the Serpents' fans loud and boisterous, their taunts and jeers a constant hum in the background.

Rinne leans in, his voice low. "Game's gonna be a bloody one."

Nieminen snorts. "Nothing like a little bad blood to get the crowd going."

Rinne and I smirk at one another. Nieminen was a legend back in his playing days, a brute on the ice. He drew more than his fair share of blood, but he always backed it up with points on the board.

My gaze drifts over the ice, taking in our players as they run through their drills. They're focused, intense, the gravity of playing their biggest rival on enemy turf weighing on them.

And then my eyes find Viktor.

He's in the net, stretching, his long, lean body contorted into a full split. I swallow hard, my fingers curling into fists in my pockets.

It's not unusual for goalies to be flexible, but the sight of him like that, spread out and open . . . it sends a jolt of heat through me, a flash of desire I can't quite suppress.

Three nights ago, after our interaction in the alleyway, I barely made it into the shower before I was fisting my cock. And then again the next morning, waking hard and aching.

He was right when he called me out, when he threw my bullshit back in my face, because the truth is, I do want him in the most feral way. And the more he pushes, the harder it is to resist him. Like the fucking fact I should be infuriated he's been spying on me in my own home.

Except, I can't help but wonder what he's seen.

Has he seen me naked? And if so, did he like it?

"You good?" Rinne's voice snaps me out of my thoughts, his brow raised in question.

I clear my throat, dragging my gaze away from Viktor. "Yeah, just not sure what to expect. Hoping Henneman's ready for this."

"This game will test what he's made of, if he's ready to be a Titan. The team will be watching him too."

The Titans' players are tough, but I've learned they also weed out those who can't hold up. Rumors claim accidents happen, but mostly, from what I gather, they just bully whoever they want off the team until that player eventually quits.

I glance over at Knight, who's eyeing Henneman. Knight's put the rookie into the boards a few times, even during practice. And full force no less.

While Henneman remains quiet, he hasn't backed down. In my book that shows character.

Rinne chuckles suddenly, nodding toward the ice. "Looks like you've got an admirer."

I follow his gaze to see Killian Blackwell, the Serpents' captain, glaring at me from across the rink. His eyes are hard, his jaw set, a clear challenge in his stance.

"What's his deal?" I mutter, meeting his stare with a cool one of my own.

"Probably just being overprotective of Reed."

Reed is stretching alongside Walsh. He seems more at ease around me, less skittish. He even came to me for advice on his puck handling. He's still recovering, and some things he's relearning how to do at the same level he used to do them.

Nieminen calls the team over, going over strategy and reminding them the Serpents are going to be coming after them. After, he turns to Reed. "You ease up on your partner out there, or I'll bench your ass so fast your head will spin."

"Might need to bench him for going too hard. Fighting's foreplay for them," Viktor says, causing half the team to snicker.

"Says the asshat with the new necklace." Reed points to the bruises on Viktor's throat.

Bruises I put there.

My stomach twists, a sour taste in my mouth. I hadn't meant to hurt him, to leave marks. I'd thought he was Noah and lost control for a moment.

But Viktor just basks in the moment, tilting his chin up with a proud glint in his eyes, as if he's showcasing the bruises. "What can I say? I like it rough."

The night in my office, I'd marked him then too, in a way. Painted his face with my cum.

But this . . . this is different. I don't like causing pain, don't like to leave marks, even if my tastes do run toward the rougher side.

Rinne shakes his head, laughing. "Surprised he's cracking jokes. Novotny's been prickly as a cactus lately. Probably needs to work out some frustration."

A smirk tugs at my lips. Well, fuck me sideways. Did the brat finally listen? Did he follow through on not touching himself?

The puck drops, the crowd roars, and it steals my full attention. The Titans and Serpents collide immediately, bodies slamming into each other, sticks clashing like swords.

I lean forward, tracking the puck as it zips across the ice. "Knight, watch your left side! Henneman, push up—support the play!"

The Serpents are relentless, their offense a battering ram against our defense. They push and push, searching for a crack, a weakness to exploit. Then Blackwell's on a breakaway, skating hard toward the goal. My heart leaps into my throat as he winds up for the shot, the puck leaving his stick like a bullet.

But Viktor's a wall of determination and skill. He slides across the crease, his leg extending in a perfect split. The puck ricochets off his pad, bouncing harmlessly away.

"Helluva save," Rinne says beside me, his voice filled with admiration. "Kid's got instincts you can't teach."

"He sure does."

The game continues, the minutes ticking by in a haze of adrenaline and sweat. The Titans fight hard, but the Serpents match them stride for stride.

In the offensive zone, Reed and Blackwell lock into one other, trading checks and stealing the puck from each other, neither willing to give an inch.

"Those two are really trying to outdo each other every shift," Rinne says as he tracks the play. "Fucking Novotny's right."

Reed gets control and passes to Walsh, who finally scores.

As the line heads back to the bench, Reed shoots Blackwell a snarky grin. "Suck it, loser."

"You'll be sucking it later." Blackwell gives him the finger before hopping over the boards.

The game gets chippy in the third period, the Serpents desperate to even the score. One of their forwards picks a fight with Henneman, breaking his nose and leaving him in a heap on the ice. Knight just watches, a cold look in his eye, as if assessing whether Henneman is worth stepping in for.

But Viktor is on fire, making save after impossible save. He's a marvel to watch, his reflexes lightning quick, his focus absolute.

Rinne leans over. "The Islanders are going to be damn lucky to have him. Though maybe he should wait until his rights are up. Test the waters as a free agent. Probably could land a better deal, a better team."

The thought makes my stomach clench, a cold fist squeezing my heart. Viktor, playing for another team. Being somewhere far away, out of reach.

It shouldn't bother me, but it does. More than I care to admit.

Before I can dwell on it, the final horn sounds, signaling the end of the game, our team pulling out a victory by one point.

On the way to the locker room, Viktor throws an arm over Reed's shoulder. "You and Kill coming to Vortex tonight?"

Reed shrugs, a half-smile on his face. "Depends. If Kill's gonna be a sore loser, might need to stay home and cheer him up."

Viktor laughs, but then he glances back at me. There's a challenge in his eyes, a provocation. He turns back to his friend. "He's not the only one who needs to let off some steam. Might need to find someone tonight to wreck my hole."

The fucking brat. He's trying to get a rise out of me, trying to push my buttons.

And damn him, it's working.

Because the thought of him grinding on some stranger in a club, letting another man's hands roam his body . . . it makes me see red, makes me want to put my fist through the wall.

He wants to play games, fine. But he'd better be ready for the consequences.

Because I'm done holding back.

Viktor

CHAPTER TEN

The bass thrums through my body, pulsing in time with my heartbeat as Eli and I weave through the crowd, the scent of alcohol and perfume thick in the air. I scan the room, searching for our friends, and spot them at our usual table, tucked away in the corner.

Connor's got his tongue down some girl's throat. Think she's the same chick from the gala at the beginning of the season. Zach's just scanning the room while rando guy's sucking his dick. Poor soul, if the schmuck knows what's good for him, he'll run away.

"Hey, look who came to hang out." Jackson half stands and gives Eli a hug. "Thought you were avoiding us all. Or only tolerated us because of Petrov."

At the mention of Alexei, Eli slouches, so I throw an arm around his shoulders, pulling him in for a side hug. "How're you holding up, with my dumbass cousin being gone?"

Eli's face falls, his eyes going distant as he drops onto the red leather sofa. "It's tough, not gonna lie. I miss him like crazy."

"He'll be back before you know it. And just think of the reunion sex." I shoot a smirk at Jackson. "Maybe you can go lay on his roommate's bed and pretend you're sleeping."

"Oh, fuck you." Jackson points at Eli. "Why don't you just tell your boyfriend you like a level of exhibitionism instead of having him threatening to kick my ass all the time."

Killian growls, looking between the three of us before settling on his boyfriend. "Fuckface, don't even think about sleeping at Eli's. If you do, it'll be your ass getting the belt."

We all laugh, even Connor who breaks away from sucking face. And I'm glad Eli is even laughing.

"What's he doing here?" Zach juts his chin toward the far end of the bar across the room.

I turn and look over my shoulder, swallowing the whimper that nearly escapes. Beckett. He's sitting at the bar, a glass of amber liquid in front of him. And he's staring right at me, his eyes dark and intense.

Eli looks at me with that worried mama bird expression. "Isn't that your assistant coach?"

"Yup."

"Are you still harassing the poor guy? You know there are rules against faculty getting involved with students?"

I can't help but flash a wicked grin. "Too late for that. Already had his dick in my mouth."

"Why am I not surprised?" Zach takes a swig of his drink, clearly annoyed.

After the night in the alley, I approached Beckett when practice was through, asking why I couldn't get off. Mostly hoping he'd do it for me. The bastard said one word.

Punishment.

So, when the game against the Serpents ended, I purposely dropped where I was going, wanting my grumpy coach to hear.

I just didn't expect him to show up. But this might work out even better because I'm frustrated as fuck. And I also have no idea why I'm even following his stupid rule.

I get up from the table and go to the bar, my gaze locked on a target. He's a big guy, all muscle and bulk.

"Hey there, handsome," I purr, sliding up next to him. "Wanna dance?"

The guy turns, looking me up and down, then grins, his hand sliding over my hip to the small of my back. "Lead the way."

I peek over his shoulder toward Becks, who's watching, jaw clenched tight. There's a storm brewing in those dark eyes, a barely contained fury that sends a shiver down my spine.

Out on the dance floor, we move to the music, our bodies grinding together. This guy's solid as a brick wall, his muscles hard, his thighs like tree trunks.

But he's not the one I truly want.

Someone bumps into me, pushing me farther into the beefcake. He takes the opportunity to wrap his arms around my waist, but his dumb hands continue sliding lower until he's palming my ass.

Oh, fuck no.

This dance is to make Beckett jealous, not have some low class ox grope me.

I grab his forearms and lift them. "Don't take what's not offered."

My body tenses, eyes blinking. Fuck me. Did I just recite the dumb shit Beckett told me?

Ugh.

"Come on, baby. Why else did you ask me to dance?" He follows up by palming my ass again and squeezing hard enough to make me grimace.

"Wrong move asshole." I slam my head forward, my forehead connecting with his nose, a sickening crunch following. He reels back, blood pouring down his face, his eyes wide with shock and pain. "Told you not to touch without permission." I laugh, the sound sharp and manic in my own ears.

But before I can savor the moment, he lunges at me. "Fucking slut."

I step back, bringing my hands up to guard my face and throw a cross, except the jerk goes flying sideways.

"Walk away." Beckett's voice is deep and gravelly.

The idiot must be short a few brain cells because he swings wildly. Beckett dodges and I just roll my eyes. Anyone who's even had an iota of training can slip those haymakers.

Problem is, he swung at my man. Or soon to be my man. Or the person I will convince to be my man.

Dropping low and sweeping the guy's legs out from under him, he goes down hard, and I grab his wrist, placing him in a wrist lock. "Next time you try to touch what's mine, I'll cut your fucking hand off."

To make my point, I wrench his wrist, feeling the bones snap.

The crowd has parted around us, everyone staring in shock and awe. I focus my attention back on Beckett and give him a cheeky grin, cocking my head to the side. "Fancy meeting you here. You following me now?"

Instead of responding, he crosses the distance between us in three long strides, then grabs me around the waist and throws me over his shoulder like a sack of potatoes.

"Put me down, you caveman!"

"Had enough of your shit tonight," he says as he tightens his grip around my thighs, making his way through the crowd.

"This is so embarrassing." The words are barely out of my mouth when a sting of pain radiates over my left butt cheek. Did he just? I twist, trying to meet his eyes and glare at him, but he just faces forward and spanks me again.

When I look back at the table where my friends are sitting, Eli's smiling so wide I can see his teeth from here. And he's giving me double thumbs up. Jackson and Killian are laughing their asses off, while Connor just shakes his head.

But Zach looks . . . angry. He even pushes away the loser who's still sucking him off.

That can't be right.

Just hope they're all smart enough to make sure Eli gets home before my cousin ends up making a trip to Crestwood to murder us all.

Beckett

CHAPTER ELEVEN

The ride back to my apartment is relatively quick, more so because I had the bike going over 100 mph, mostly to calm myself down. While Viktor's bratty side seriously pushed some limits, I also caught the way he backed up when that jackass's hands first started to dip lower.

What's unsettling is not knowing what length Viktor will go to for attention. There's no denying he has mine. But then what? He moves on?

Why am I even thinking about this? It's not like I want something serious with him. Not when my life is starting to feel like it's getting back on track.

I know I'm playing with fire by giving into him right now but, as he pointed out, I already crossed the line. And maybe fucking him will get it out of both of our systems. He'll move on and turn his attention to someone else.

Throwing the door open to my apartment, I pull him inside, then slam the door and pin him against it. "You think you can handle me because of a little throat fuck?

Well, you're about to find out what you've really gotten yourself into."

I crash my mouth down on his, devouring him as I rip his shirt open, buttons flying everywhere. My tongue dominates his as I grapple with his belt, then pants. When I yank the zipper, it rips and I know I probably just destroyed his really expensive suit.

Oh, well. I'm sure he has the money to replace it.

He moans and whimpers into my mouth, rocking against me as he kicks off his shoes, then pants.

"Such a needy slut. Is this because you haven't gotten off for a few days? Or are you always this way?"

"I . . . you. Want so bad."

Pulling back, I pin him with a glare. "You smell like him."

"Who?"

"The asshole you were dancing with." I grab his arm and lead him toward the bathroom. "Want the scent of that cheap cologne gone."

"Jealous?"

When I look over my shoulder at him, he's smirking, like a fucking brat. Oh, I'm going to put that mouth of his to good use. But a shower is in order first because that citrus smell is turning my stomach.

"Thought I was *off limits*?"

"I'm way past giving a fuck right now, Chaos."

Pushing Viktor into the bathroom, I flick on the light, then back him up against the vanity. My fingers hook into the waistband of his boxers and I pull them down.

What I don't expect is for the arrogant goalie to freeze up. Not sure why. Because, fuck, his cock is gorgeous—long, thick, and mouthwateringly hard.

"Uh, you know what. You're right. Maybe we should think this through. Can't risk having you get fired." There's a tremble to his voice, and he's looking all over.

I stand, then take step back, unsure what the fuck just happened. But as I look back down, raking my hand through my hair, hard as fuck and equally confused, my eyes are drawn to the thin, jagged silver line marring the side of his buttock.

When I reach for his hip, he backs up as far as he can get. "Viktor—"

"Think I should go."

Except when he bends to grab his boxers, more of his ass is on display. More scars are on display.

"Chaos?"

He straightens slowly, eyes downcast.

I close whatever distance is between us. "Who did this to you?"

Viktor nibbles on his bottom lip. "It's nothing. Just some fun gone wrong."

Like fuck.

Lifting his chin with my forefinger, I make sure our gazes lock. "You've been stalking me, flirting with me, pushing my buttons, and now that you're about to get what you want, you're trying to run out of here. So, no Chaos, this isn't nothing. Who marked your beautiful body like this?"

He throws a dismissive hand in the air, the smile on his face fake. It doesn't reach his eyes, and it's too tight. "It's not a big deal. Just a bit of kinky sex."

"Did you like it?" My voice is calmer because the last thing I want to do is kink shame.

"The sex was great."

"Not what I asked."

His shoulders slump a bit. "No."

"Did you have a safe word? Why didn't he . . . or she stop?"

He chuckles. It's soft and low. "I'm gay, so it wasn't a woman. And it was new and thrilling and I got caught up and Zach—"

"Knight!" My voice booms and I swear people across the street must be able to hear me. "Fucking Zachary Knight did this to you?"

Viktor's lip trembles, his eyes wide and wet. "Please don't make a big deal. He just got carried away. It's in the past."

"Can't promise that."

"He's my friend." Viktor steps forward, practically curling into me. "He didn't mean it. I've gotten past it. Please let it go."

I close my eyes, taking a deep breath. "Fine. Now get in the shower."

He goes willingly, more subdued, the heated moment between us gone. As he steps into the stall I really look at the marks on him. Some are definitely from knife play, but others appear to be from a whip. I've seen shoddy whip work, mostly from inexperienced people or those who were high or drunk.

Neither fit who Knight is.

Which could only mean he opened Viktor's skin on purpose.

I swallow hard and step in behind Viktor, turning on the water and letting it heat up before gently pushing him under the hot spray.

For someone so confident, so brazen, I'm starting to wonder if maybe he's not as self-assured as he lets on.

"Too hot?"

He shakes his head. "It's perfect. You going to wash me? Pamper me?"

I reach past him to the soap dispenser on the wall, pressing the lever to fill my hand with a rich, fragrant body wash. "That's exactly what I'm going to do."

For fuck's sake, he's basking in this, his eyes half-closed and a content smile playing on his lips.

I chuckle as I sink to one knee, the other bent with my foot flat on the shower floor. Reaching out, I take hold of Viktor's right ankle, guiding his foot to rest on my thigh. Starting at his calf, I wash and massage his lean muscles, relishing the feel of his skin under my hands.

Slowly, I work my way up, kneading the defined muscle of his thigh, noting how different his build is from the defensemen and forwards.

Viktor is lean, his musculature evenly distributed rather than bulky. But there's no denying his strength, the coiled power in his long limbs. He's built for speed, for agility. A body honed to perfection for his role on the ice.

And fuck if it isn't the most beautiful thing I've ever seen.

When I've thoroughly washed his right leg, I guide his foot back to the floor, then tap his other ankle. "Other leg, Chaos."

He obeys without hesitation, lifting his left foot to rest on my thigh. I start the process again, washing and massaging from calf to thigh.

My hands linger, my touch shifting from cleansing to caressing. I trace the lines of his muscles, the jut of his hip bone, the curve of his ass.

Viktor's head falls back against the wall, a low moan escaping. "Beckett . . ."

The way he says my name, rough and needy, makes my cock throb. I want to hear him say it again, want him to scream it.

I stand, reaching past him for more soap, then run my hands over his torso, my fingers tracing the ridges of his abs before washing his arms, admiring the way his veins pop under his skin.

"Turn around. Keep your hands on the wall."

He obeys instantly, looking at me over his shoulder with hooded eyes. I let my gaze roam over the expanse of his back, drinking in the sight of him.

"Knew you liked me," he purrs, his hips swaying slightly as his gaze drops to my cock. "Bet you can't wait to push that thick monster into my hole."

"Shut it." I let my soapy fingers dip between the cheeks of his ass, and he pushes his hips back, a whine reverberating deep in his throat. My cock twitches at the sound.

Leaning forward, I nip at the shell of his ear as my finger circles his tight hole. "So fucking needy. So desperate for my touch."

But even as I tease him, I take my time, savoring every moment. This isn't just about cleaning him. It's about erasing every trace of that cheap cologne, replacing it with my scent.

When he's fully rinsed, I drop to my knees behind him, my hands spreading him open. I press open-mouthed kisses to the base of his spine, my teeth grazing his skin, my lips kissing every scar.

My tongue traces a hot, wet path to his hole and when I reach it, I dive in, licking a broad stripe over the furled muscle. The taste of him, musky and masculine, explodes on my tongue.

Viktor's knees buckle, and he scrabbles at the slick tiles. "Fuck!"

I growl against his skin, the vibrations making him tremble. My tongue delves deep, fucking into him with rough, demanding strokes.

"Beckett, fuck, yes!" Viktor babbles, his voice high and breathy as he pushes back against me. "Don't stop, fuck, please don't stop . . ."

"That's it, Chaos. Show me what a dirty boy you are."

And he does, whining and whimpering as I lick and suck at his hole, alternating between broad, flat strokes and pointed jabs.

When his legs start to shake, I stop, then stand, turning him around to face me. "On your knees. Time to apologize for dancing with that jackass."

Viktor sinks to the shower floor without hesitation, his eyes locked on my aching cock. He leans in, nuzzling the hard length, his soft lips brushing the sensitive skin.

"Fuck," I hiss, my hand fisting in his wet hair. "Stop teasing and suck me."

"So impatient, Becks. Don't you want me to savor it?"

"What I want . . ." I growl, tightening my grip. ". . . is for you to put that bratty mouth to better use."

Viktor grins, then parts his lips, taking just the head into his hot, wet mouth.

I groan, my hips bucking. "Deeper. Show me how sorry you are."

Relaxing his throat, he swallows me down until his nose presses against my pelvis. I hold him there, reveling in the tight, fluttering heat of his throat.

"Never going to forget how you look with your mouth full of my cock." I rasp, my thumb stroking over his hollowed cheek. "So. Fucking. Beautiful."

Viktor whimpers, the sound muffled around my flesh. He looks up at me, his eyes watering.

"You like having your mouth stuffed with me, don't you?" I rock my hips in a shallow thrust. "Nod for me, Chaos."

He does, as best he can with his mouth stretched wide. The sight makes my balls tighten, pleasure coiling hot and heavy in my gut. Grabbing onto his head with both hands for leverage, I thrust into him roughly, using his mouth how I like. He takes it beautifully, his throat working around me just like last time, his fingers digging into my thighs.

My orgasm builds fast, too fast, and I pull out abruptly. Viktor cries at the loss, his lips swollen and slick with spit. "Not yet. I want to be inside you when I come. Want to feel you squeezing my cock."

"Fucking finally. Thought I would waste away to dust before you decided to wreck my ass."

Rolling my eyes, I scoop him up and carry him to the bed.

He laughs, a rich, self-satisfied sound. "Oh, so it's the princess carry, huh? Guess I'm precious cargo now."

I press my lips into a thin line, fighting back a smirk as I carry him into the bedroom, then toss the brat onto the bed, enjoying the little "oof" he makes as he bounces on the mattress. He props himself up on his elbows, his legs falling open in clear invitation.

"Well, come on then, big boy," he taunts, his eyes glinting with mischief. "Show me what you've got."

I slap the inside of his thigh, making him yelp. "On your hands and knees, facing the cheval floor mirror."

"Ooh, kinky. You want me to watch while you take me apart?" He winks, then arranges himself on the bed, presenting his perfect ass to me.

"Always have to run your mouth, huh?" I slap his ass hard enough to turn the skin pink. "And no. I don't want you looking at me. I want you to see how beautiful you are. How good you look getting fucked."

Something flickers in his eyes. Viktor needs attention just as much as he needs oxygen. He'll do anything for it, and based off his earlier admission, I can't help but wonder if he knows what he genuinely likes.

Or if he goes along with whatever his partner wants to guarantee he gets the attention he craves.

I grab lube and a condom from the nightstand, quickly preparing us, then I kneel behind him, lining up and pushing in with one smooth, relentless thrust.

Viktor's mouth falls open, a broken moan escaping as he's filled. His arms tremble, struggling to hold himself up.

I reach out, fisting a hand in his hair and yanking his head up. "Watch yourself, Chaos. Watch as I destroy this ass."

His eyes are locked on his reflection, wide and dark with lust as the sound of skin-on-skin echoes in the room. His body jolts with every thrust, his cock swaying heavy and hard between his legs.

"Look at you taking my cock so well, like you were made for it."

His cheeks are flushed, his lips swollen and parted as he pushes his hips back to meet my thrusts. One of his hands drifts to his chest, fingers tugging on a nipple.

"That's it. Pinch them, play with them. Show me how you like it."

He does, plucking and pulling, and putting on a show, whether he realizes it or not, performing for his own reflection.

And fuck. What a show it is.

I drink in the sight of him, the sound of his moans, the feel of his body tight and hot around me. It's almost too much, almost overwhelming in its intensity.

But I don't slow down, don't hold back. I can't, not when he's looking like that, not when he's falling apart so beautifully.

His whole body shudders, a broken moan tearing from his throat, his hand flying to his dripping cock. "Feels so good, so fucking good . . ."

"That's it. Play with your cock. I want to see you come while I'm buried inside you."

He strokes himself hard, fast, relentlessly. "Fuck. Oh, fuck, Beckett! I'm gonna . . . Fuck, I'm coming!"

His ass clamps down around me as he spills over his fist, his whole body shaking with the force of his orgasm. The sensation pushes me over the edge, and I bury myself to the hilt, grinding against his prostate as I empty myself into the condom, a guttural groan tearing from my throat.

Viktor whimpers, still rocking back against me, milking every last drop.

I collapse on top of him as we struggle to catch our breath, both panting, sweat-slick, and spent, our hearts racing in tandem.

"Fuck, that was . . ." he trails off, seeming at a loss for words. A rarity for him.

"Incredible," I finish, carefully pulling out, then sitting up to remove the condom and tie it off. "You were incredible."

He rolls onto his back and hums, a satisfied smile on his face. "I know."

"Brat." I roll my eyes, but I can't stop the fondness that swells in my chest. Even post-orgasm, he's still a brat.

My brat.

Fuck.

I shake my head as I get out of bed and pad into the bathroom. After disposing of the condom, I walk to the cabinet and, just as I open the door to grab a washcloth, a white ball of fur bursts out. "Goddammit, Mouse!"

My heart's beating a million miles an hour as I mumble, wetting the cloth with warm water. Shaking my head and taking a few deep breaths, I return to the bedroom to find Viktor fast asleep.

Carefully, I clean him up, wiping away the sweat, lube, and cum. After, I toss the cloth aside and arrange him more comfortably on the bed before sliding in behind him. I pull him close, his back to my chest, savoring the way he fits against me.

As I listen to the steady rhythm of his breathing, a sinking realization settles in my gut.

I'm fucked. Completely and utterly fucked.

This was supposed to be a one-time thing, a way to get the infuriating goalie out of my system, an itch to scratch and then move on, going back to our roles of coach and player.

But now, with his warmth seeping into my skin, his scent filling my lungs . . . I know once will never be enough.

I want more. I want everything.

And that wanting, that bone-deep need . . .

It might just cost me everything.

Viktor

CHAPTER TWELVE

Scrubbing my face, I stretch my legs and toes as I roll onto my back. My body is deliciously sore, burning in all the right places. Can't recall the last time I've been fucked like that. Actually, I don't think I ever have been.

Used yes.

But where my own pleasure was taken into consideration . . . no, no one ever put in the effort. Or maybe I never let them, too focused on what they wanted in order to keep them around.

As my eyelids flutter open and my brain starts coming online, I register the weight of an arm across my abdomen and the sleepy grumbling.

Oh, fuck me.

Beckett.

I'm still at his place, tucked into his bed. He didn't kick me out after we fucked. He . . . he let me stay.

Another thing that's never happened. Usually, I'm out the door before the sweat even dries, a hasty "Thanks" thrown over my shoulder as I leave.

Except for those few times I tried my hand at *relationships*.

Being discarded like a sex toy didn't compare to being told I was, "too much" and "too intense."

My muscles tense.

Of all the things I've been called, those two are the ones that cut the deepest—triggers, as my former therapist once said.

The others—psychopath, unhinged, lunatic, crazy—I own, made them a part of who I am.

I blink rapidly, swallowing past the lump in my throat. It's only a matter of time before I overwhelm Becks and he leaves.

Except, he's mine, so I need to figure out a way to make him stay, to accept I'm worth the headache I give.

I slip out of bed, grabbing my boxers from the floor. They're the only piece of clothing Beckett didn't absolutely destroy last night. The memory of him ripping my shirt, the feral look in his eyes . . . it makes me shiver, my dick twitching and wanting more.

Down, boy. We've got work to do.

I pad quietly toward my pants on the floor by the front door, then grab my phone. Nothing like an internet search to spark some ideas on how to prove my worth as a boyfriend.

Wait, boyfriend?

Slow your roll, Novotny. One night of mind-blowing sex does not a relationship make.

I flop onto the couch and unlock the screen. "Holy shit."

My hand flies up over my mouth, worried I was too loud.

Forty text messages.

What the hell did I miss? My stomach knots up. Did my friends need me and I wasn't there? Quickly, I open the Bottoms Up group chat, hoping Eli is okay, especially considering the number of notifications.

Feisty Mouse:

Made it home.

Jackson:

Novy, let us know you're okay.

Feisty Mouse:

He's fine. Did you see your coach spank him?

Jackson:

Don't start Mr. Likes-a-Red-Bottom.

Killian:

He's not the only one.

Jackson:

Shut it before I get my belt.

Feisty Mouse:

Stop. That's not fair. Especially when my boyfriend is away.

Feisty Mouse:

Viktor, just let us know you're ok. That he didn't hurt you.

Jackson:

Feisty Mouse:

Sorry, Jackson. But I'm worried.

Killian:

He's fine. But why is Jackson getting a shit ton of messages from Alexei. Do I really need to worry about Alexei skinning me alive?

Feisty Mouse:

Ignore my dumbass boyfriend.

Oh, Eli is dead. He invited them both to the chat. And they both accepted, even knowing the rule was only one of them could join.

Fucktards.

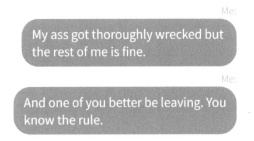

I tap on the string of messages from my cousin, knowing automatically he's like an angry bull right now.

He goes on and on, but I don't bother responding. I get it, he's too far in case anything goes wrong. And he's right. He entrusted me to keep Eli safe. But I'm not his bodyguard and I know my cousin set up a shit ton of cameras in Feisty Mouse's dorm room.

Closing the app, I open the web browser and start searching for ideas on how to prove I'm worthy to Beckett: make breakfast, surprise picnic dates, blah, blah, and boring blah. But then I vaguely remember him yelling something about a mouse last night.

Now, getting rid of a little rodent fucker would definitely help make my assistant coach fall head over heels in love with me.

I start researching how to go about catching this pest. According to some top sites, the best places to start are at the bases of kitchen cabinets, voids in and behind large kitchen appliances, and voids near heat sources.

Getting off the couch, I head to the kitchen, because I'm going to catch this furry little shit if it's the last thing I do.

Nothing near the radiator, not even a tiny hole. Bases of the cabinets are next. I groan as I drop to my hands and knees, crawling around. If my friends could see me now.

No evidence so far.

But when I sit back on my heels, a pair of mismatched eyes stare down at me, one green, one blue. Just like Beckett's. "Jesus, fuck!"

The white furball starts yowling like the mother of all angry cats.

Didn't know Becks had a pet, one that's not supposed to be here. The building owner—a by-the-rules, animal-hating dictator—would flip if he knew. Yeah, I made it my business to know every detail about this place from the layout to obtaining a copy of the lease.

Which has a strict no-pet policy.

I narrow my eyes and stare at it. "Make some noise next time, would you?"

It hisses, tail lashing.

Oh, this one sure has some attitude.

I lean in closer, my nose scrunching. "Why does he even have you? What kind of cat are you letting a mouse run around? Isn't that what you're bred for?"

The cat growls, then bats me in the face three times.

Note to self: do not challenge a cat face to face. I should've known better, but most of the time I've learned every lesson the hard way because I do in fact fuck around and find out.

I roll my eyes, getting to my feet. "Some hunter you are, letting rodents run around like they pay rent."

The white furball looks thoroughly unimpressed. With a disdainful sniff, it turns its back on me, tail held high.

"Fine. Be that way. But don't come crying to me when the mice take over."

I resume searching again, grumbling under my breath. Stupid cat, stupid mouse, stupid Beckett and his stupidly perfect dick that's turned my brain to mush.

After a few fruitless minutes, I sit back against the cabinets, sighing. The cat's now lounging on the counter, watching me with a bored expression.

"You could help, you know." I point an accusing finger. "But no, you just want to sit there and judge me. Lazy ass."

She yawns, showing off her sharp little teeth. I swear she's laughing at me.

"Guess the supervisor's supervising, huh?"

A snort from behind makes me twist around. Beckett's leaning against the doorway, his arms crossed over his bare chest—his very muscular, very bite-able chest. "What are you doing?"

"I was, uh . . . looking for the mouse?" It comes out as a question, my confidence wilting under his gaze.

His eyebrows shoot up, a smirk tugging at his lips. "The mouse?"

I nod, gesturing to the cat as I get to my feet. "Yeah, but this one's not being very helpful."

Beckett laughs, a rich, warm sound that makes my toes curl. He pushes off the doorframe, coming over to scoop the cat into his arms.

"Viktor, meet Mouse." He scratches the cat under its chin. "Mouse, meet Viktor."

I stare at him. Blink. Stare some more. "I'm sorry, what? You named your cat . . . *Mouse*?"

He shrugs, still grinning.

I shake my head slowly, my lips twitching. "And they call me unhinged. Seriously, Beckett, what is wrong with you?"

He sets Mouse down, stepping closer to me. His hands find my hips, his thumbs rubbing small circles into my skin. "You know, if I actually had a rodent in here I'd just call an exterminator."

"Was just trying to be helpful."

Beckett chuckles and shakes his head. "Sometimes you're just too much."

My body stiffens, muscles tensing, and I force a smile that feels fake even to me. "You know I like the accolades."

But my act doesn't work. His brows furrow as he studies my face. "What was that? What happened?"

I blink a few times, trying to figure out what to say, but the words just won't come.

"Viktor?"

"It's nothing."

"Bullshit." He backs me up against the kitchen table, then lifts me to sit on it and steps between my legs. "Talk to me."

I shrug, looking down at nothing in particular. "Just kinda tired of being told I'm too much. Too intense. Too *overwhelming*."

He tilts my chin up until our gazes meet. "Chaos, you just shine too brightly for most people. Don't dim your light because they can't handle it."

I snort. "Yeah, well . . . What about you?"

"I'm perfectly fine wearing a pair of sunglasses."

Not the response I was expecting. At all. And when he smiles so big his eyes crinkle at the sides, my smart mouth has to get in the way. "Is that what they're calling cataracts these days?"

Beckett grips behind my knees and pulls me flush against him. "You calling me old?"

I smirk. "If the shoe fits."

His fingers trail up to my waist, then dip into the waistband of my boxer briefs. "Take these off."

I lift my hips and remove my underwear, my dick already hard and leaking.

"Now, turn around, chest and knees on the table. Ass up."

Oh, this sounds like fun. "Going to fuck me before school, Becks? Make me so sore I'll be thinking about you during all my classes?"

He doesn't answer, only stands there with a steady gaze and a slight smirk, his arms relaxed at his sides as he waits, so I get into position. Although, I'm not sure how he intends to fuck me like this. I'm up too high.

"Reach back and spread your cheeks for me."

The whimper that erupts cracks at the end, all high pitched and filthy. I swallow hard as I turn my head to the side, then reach back and grab my ass, spreading myself wide.

"So fucking pretty. Can't wait to feast on you and make you all sloppy."

Before I can respond, he buries his face in me, his beard scraping against my sensitive skin in a way that adds to the intensity of his warm, wet tongue pressing against my hole.

"God, fuck. Oh, fuck." My voice sounds so filthy and needy, my fingers digging into my skin so hard as I spread myself wider that it'll probably leave bruises.

Beckett chuckles as he continues to lap at my hole, short, soft licks across before plunging with the tip of his tongue, dipping inside until I push back against him.

"Such a needy brat." He pulls away, then sucks my balls before tracing his tongue back up my crack. "Look at you shaking already, making such a mess on my table."

"More. Now."

And he obliges, sucking my hole and plunging his firm tongue back inside, fucking me with it over and over until I'm writhing against his face. Beckett's eating me out like I'm his last fucking meal . . . or his first.

"I'm gonna come. Beckett, oh, fuck. I'm gonna blow."

He instantly pulls away and I wail at the loss of contact. But he flips me onto my back, spins me around, then climbs onto the table and straddles my face. I have no idea when he pulled off his pants but his red, angry crown is suddenly pushing into my mouth.

I open without hesitating, tasting his precum and moaning as I take him deeper.

"That's it, Chaos. Suck my cock. Suck it like you need my cum to survive."

And I do, swirling my tongue around his hard, hot length as I hollow out my cheeks. He starts driving into me and when I gag, he moans low.

"Love the way you choke on me. Your fucking mouth is heaven. Take it, baby."

I grab onto the back of his thighs when he pushes into my throat as I gag and sputter around him. Beckett's not taking it easy, getting rougher by the second . . . and I love it.

I arch, my dick aching and hurting, getting harder with each of his grunts and raspy groans, silently begging for him to get me off too.

The table scrapes against the floor, the sound mixing with the sloppy wet gurgles I make trying to relax my throat with each of his thrusts.

"Such a filthy boy. Look at your cock, drooling all over your stomach." His tongue licks across my abs as he pushes himself all the way in until his pelvis is flush against my face. "That's it, Chaos. Fuck, swallow again, contract that throat around my cock. Yes, baby. Just like that."

I squeeze his thighs, my body on fire, but my consciousness grows fuzzy around the edges. He pulls out and I suck in a breath, a thread of saliva connecting my lips to his crown.

"Want more?"

I nod, opening wide.

He fills my mouth once again, but this time he takes me into his. He sucks just as intensely as he thrusts and seconds later I'm flooding his mouth, whining around his dick as my whole body contracts and I come. He doesn't ease up until spurts of his hot cum jet onto my tongue.

The long groan Beckett makes as he orgasms with my dick still in his mouth, vibrates throughout my whole body. He pulls free, then turns to face me, gripping my jaw and forcing my mouth open.

He leans down, feeding me my own cum, then pulls back, running his thumb over my bottom lip. "Swallow."

After I do, he hops off the table. "Time to get ready for class."

I sit up, mind hazy. "I . . . No clothes."

He brushes my hair away from my eyes, then kisses my forehead. "You can wear mine."

Beckett

CHAPTER THIRTEEN

Watching Viktor wilt when I mentioned he was too much made my chest hurt in ways I didn't expect. Sure, I care about how people feel, but what caught me by surprise was the strength of my reaction.

Same way those scars made me want to ride back to the club last night and rip Zachary Knight's throat out, especially after Viktor admitted he hadn't liked it. Which also means, I have to be careful with him, pay attention to what he actually enjoys versus what he may be doing solely for my benefit.

My focus lingers on the brat as he walks into the rink wearing one of my sweatshirts and a pair of my joggers, both a bit too big. But fuck. He looks sexy as hell in my clothes. And I already know I'm not getting that sweatshirt back, not with the way he keeps lifting his arm and smelling the sleeve.

I may have sprayed some of my cologne on it before giving it to him. While physically marking someone isn't my thing, that doesn't mean I won't do it in other ways.

My eyes close as I take a deep breath and shake my head.

This thing with Viktor is a bad idea on so many levels, but staying away isn't an option, not after fucking him, tasting him, and falling asleep with him in my arms.

Problem is, as much as I want to keep whatever we're doing a secret, my actions last night were in front of his friends. They all saw me carry him out of the club. Doubt they'd buy the excuse nothing happened, especially because there's no way Viktor will keep quiet.

And I don't want him to feel less than, like a dirty secret.

Some of my tension eased when he literally went feral the moment I brought up being worried about losing my job, like he'd nuke the damn planet if they even tried to fire me.

Yeah, he's intense. And not always in a good way, but there's no denying his intentions do appear to stem from caring. He just . . . doesn't always express it in the right ways.

"What's got you daydreaming?" Rinne hands me a cup of coffee.

"Thanks." I take a sip, then glance around the rink. "Just taking it in. Some of the guys are finally seeing me as a coach, others . . . not so sure. It's like I'm still on probation."

"For what it's worth, I think you're doing great, especially with Henneman. Kid's coming around. Looking more confident out there."

"What about Nieminen?"

Rinne lets out a full-on belly laugh. "You kidding? That man is so happy to share the migraine this team gives him. Yeah, he's snippy. But more like the way my wife just looks at me and says, 'They're all yours now' the moment I get home because she's had enough."

Not sure what that's like, the having kids part, though I used to think about it some.

Taking another sip of coffee, I look over at Rinne. He's a good dad from what I can tell. Always calls his kids before practice, shows me tons of videos. And I can appreciate it more when he occasionally complains about going from working with Viktor, then home to his son who's just as demanding for attention.

"How'd you get through to Henneman, anyway?"

I grin as I swirl my cup around. "Easy when we're both the new guys walking onto the championship team. Nerves are the same. Expectations are the same. We just have different roles."

"Gotta ask. What's with him and showers?"

Something I've noticed too. Not everyone showers at the rink, but even at away games he doesn't. Not sanitary, especially with all that sweat. Some of the players have started teasing him about it. "Not sure. Trying to figure out a way to casually bring it up."

"Tread carefully. Saw his hand start shaking one day when Knight backed him into one of the stalls. You know how some of the team is, bunch of fucking bullies."

"Knight hurt him." I clench my jaw a bit too hard.

"Not that I can tell. Outside of the one incident, I don't see Henneman backing down even when Knight goes after him on the ice."

My attention drifts over to the players getting on the ice, specifically number twenty-seven, Knight. I know exactly what he's capable of. And what makes me nearly lose my shit is when I see Viktor sidle up to the guy.

"Start warming up." Nieminen blows his whistle, then walks to us. "Harper, you got everything set up for video review later?"

"Yup. Want to get some one-on-one time with some of the newer players. Mind if I pull them early?"

"Do what you gotta do. We have a title to defend."

Rinne skates off to work with Viktor and our back-up goalie, while Nieminen works with the offense, leaving me with the defense. It takes no more than five minutes before Knight goes at Henneman like the rookie is his personal chew toy.

"Zach, focus or get the fuck off my ice." My voice is deep, my words hard. "He's not going to learn anything if he's always watching his back from one of his own."

He looks over at me, eyes practically void, the only hint of emotion the tiny lift of his upper lip. And just for good measure, he cross checks Henneman, knocking him on his ass.

"To my office now! The rest of you go with Coach Nieminen."

The team and coaches all stare, but I catch the tiny smirk on Nieminen's face. Knight slams his stick across the boards as he exits, and when I turn toward the net, Viktor's eyes bounce between me and his friend, but he doesn't lift the goalie helmet, so I can't read his expression.

Once inside the small office, I slam the door and point at Knight. "What the actual fuck is your problem! Why are you going at Henneman like that?"

"He doesn't belong here." His voice is calm, cold, and fully controlled. "Just because Crestwood let some scholarship student onto the team doesn't mean he's any good."

"Listen, you entitled prick, I never want to hear that type of shit from your mouth again toward any of your teammates. Got it? I can't control what you say to anyone else, but I protect my players so keep that shit to yourself."

He just stares, his body calm. No hint of remorse, no hint of stress. "He doesn't belong, but he'll get the message sooner or later."

The university warned me about the students here. How their families run everything. Nieminen did too, specifically mentioning Viktor and his friends. But enough is enough. I don't care how rich their parents are. I won't stand by and let this piece of shit hurt people.

I step into his space, my face inches from him. "Touch him again and you're done. Mommy and Daddy won't be able to help you."

A muscle twitches near his eye, his nostrils flaring. Seems I hit some sort of button. Good. Maybe I'm finally getting through that thick skull of his.

But then he narrows his eyes and smirks. "He'll get bored of you soon."

I jerk back, blinking.

His lips lift into even more of a venomous grin. "Then I'll touch him in whatever way I want."

Viktor.

He's talking about Viktor.

Whatever little decorum I had flies out of the window and I grab his jersey, slamming him against the wall. "Lay a finger on either Novotny or Henneman again and I will break your arms in a way they won't heal properly. You won't be so lucky next time."

The grin falls, morphing into a glare.

"I saw the marks, Zach. The scars. He didn't want that, didn't even enjoy it. And you don't even fucking care. You'll—"

"I do fucking care!"

He looks over my shoulder, his features scrunching. I turn, expecting to find Viktor, but instead find Reed, eyes wide and skin ashen.

Fuck.

I let go of Knight and step back, raking my hands through my hair. "I'm sorry. I shouldn't have done that."

"Can I go?" Knight's voice waivers, some emotion slipping through.

"Yeah."

He leaves and I drop into my office chair, keeping my distance from Reed. This is the last thing he needed to see, the last way I needed to react in front of him.

"Jackson, I'm sorry. If you want to report what you saw, I fully understand."

He clears his throat, then steps into the office, closing the door. "Knight deserved it. And well, we've been wondering what the fuck went on between him and Novy. Now I've got something to hang over Knight's head . . . you know, because Petrov has no clue and will likely kill him."

My eyes widen and I groan. "Jesus, fuck. Why are you smiling about that?"

"You have no idea how hard it is to keep Zach in line sometimes. Now I have something that might help." Jackson takes a seat in Nieminen's chair. "Anyway, I was wondering if I can talk to you about something. But I don't want Coach Nieminen to know. I'm still figuring things out, but there's something I want to get your opinion about."

"Um, sure."

He sits back, picking at the sleeve of his jersey. "And don't worry. You're just protecting your boy. It's nothing like what happened to me. I just . . . sometimes it's like a flashback. PTSD or something."

I keep quiet, partially because he's opening up, and also because I'm stuck on the way he called Viktor my boy.

My first reaction was to correct it to *my brat*.

There's also another reason, one that has me smile in a way I haven't in a while.

For the first time, I feel like a real coach, not just some new guy running drills and barking at the players.

And fuck does it feel good.

Viktor

CHAPTER FOURTEEN

Pulling up to Beckett's apartment feels weird when I'm driving the McLaren instead of the Pacifica. But the last thing I want is for anyone to find out about my stalkermobile, least of all Becks.

That man would be so angry, he might make me get rid of it.

After parking and turning off the engine, I lift my wrist to my nose, inhaling the scent coming from his heather gray sweatshirt. Hope he doesn't make me give it back. This thing is comfortable, which is why I didn't bother changing into my own clothes.

When practice ended, I returned to my dorm to get some homework done, and to interrogate Jackson for information since Zach never returned to practice. But my friend kept quiet. He wouldn't even tell me what he talked to Becks about.

Midway through my assignments, Becks texted, asking if I wanted to come over. Like I wasn't going to show up anyway. So, I prepped and took another shower before heading out.

I reach over to the passenger seat and grab my backpack. My heart beats faster, pulse thumping in my temples as I open the small front pocket and doublecheck the contents—two syringes and some Rohypnol.

Never been worried about tagging someone before, but if it doesn't go correctly, and Beckett figures out what I'm doing, I'll lose him for sure.

Once I rezip the pocket, I get out of the car and make my way to his building, then up to the second floor, texting him as I climb the stairs.

Of course, he's waiting in the doorway. "Like my clothes that much? Figured they were too cheap for you."

"You mean *my* clothes, and I own things that aren't all labels."

"Like what?"

I drop my backpack by the entrance, then kick off my shoes and hold out a foot. "My socks. They're some obscure brand."

He just shakes his head and closes the door. I turn and head for the couch when the white ball of fur comes by and I scoop the cat into my arms. It yowls and hisses, but I still pet its head. "Is Mouse a boy or girl?"

"Girl."

Sitting, I continue to hold her, and as much as she vocally complains, she's not fighting me. "Both of your eyes are the same and she's grumpy as fuck, she's a mini version of you."

Beckett sits next to me shaking his head as pulls the cat from me, placing her beside him. He grabs the back of my head and pulls me in, his mouth claiming mine. "You look good in *my* clothes."

"Well, good thing because I'm keeping my boyfriend's sweatshirt."

His body tenses and he pulls away, his face becoming serious. "Viktor, I . . . uh, this thing between us . . . it's not like that. I'm not ready for that level of commitment."

My throat tightens and I fidget with the sleeve of the sweatshirt.

He places a hand on my thigh. "Chaos, I'm sorry. I . . . Look, we're attracted to each other. And as much as I try to resist you, I can't. But a serious relationship is out of the question."

The phone on the table vibrates and a muscle near his jaw ticks when he glances quickly at it. Before he can stop me, I grab it, then hit the green button, so pissed, I don't even register the name on the screen. "Who the fuck is this?"

A male voice answers but Beckett rips the phone from my hand and hangs it up. "You crossed the line with that stunt."

"Was that Noah?"

"No, it was my brother." He releases a deep sigh, his tone clipped. "Novotny, stay out of my business with Noah."

Novotny.

Back to that now.

My eyes narrow to slits, my hands clenching into fists. "Oh, so you have a right to go after one of my friends, but I mention your what—your ex-boyfriend or is he still your boyfriend—and I'm in the wrong?"

I spring to my feet so fast it sends Mouse scurrying away. "Am I just some fucking placeholder until he moves here with you?"

"No." Beckett's voice is quiet, like a defeated whisper, as he stares at the ground. "He's dangerous. You had to notice part of Mouse's left ear missing. Noah cut it off with a pair of fucking safety scissors because he got jealous. Of my cat. He fucked around with my job, nearly got me fired. He stalked me." He looks up and glares at me for a moment before continuing. "I had to get a restraining order on him."

I sit back down next to him, then wrap my arms around his waist, laying my head against his shoulder. "Why didn't you just tell me that night in the alleyway?"

His body deflates and he hugs me back. "I don't want him making you a target too."

My body shakes as I laugh. "You have no idea what my friends and I are capable of. The last thing you need to do is worry about me."

"I've been warned about all of you, but specifics were never mentioned." He hugs me tighter, his cheek resting against the side of my head. "I understand if keeping things casual isn't what you want. But it's what I need. Getting serious, right now, with you . . . It's just too much."

Too much.

My body tenses, pulse rate spiking, and it feels as if someone's squeezing the shit out of my temples.

Isn't that always my issue? And though I try to calm down, knowing in my gut he didn't mean it that way, it resounds within my head until it pounds so fiercely I'm seeing those small flashing spots.

"I should just go home."

He tenses, pulling back to look at me. "Viktor, I didn't mean—"

"Don't." I shove him away and stand, heading straight for the door, grabbing my bag and sneakers before walking out and slamming it behind me. I practically speedwalk barefoot to my car, then drive away.

Fuck Beckett Harper for giving me hope that maybe someone could finally accept me for who I am.

Beckett

CHAPTER FIFTEEN

Viktor's wounded, has been, long before me, and carelessly using one of the phrases he told me hurts him just twisted the knife. The worst part? This is all on me. I crossed the line the moment I had Viktor down on his knees. I was the one who never made it clear this was casual when *I* decided to let it go further.

Ironically, I don't believe my own bullshit. Not with the way I react so strongly to him being upset. Or how much I hated the way he smelled like another man that night at the club. Or how I couldn't wait to see him two nights ago, pacing around like a kid on Christmas morning waiting for their parents to get up.

And it isn't even about sex.

But like everything in my life, things just go sideways, mostly of my own volition.

"You look like shit. What's going on?" Rinne asks, pulling me out of my own head.

"Don't even know where to start."

"Guy problems?" He hands me a small bag of Sour Patch Kids.

I snatch them and tear into the candy, sighing as I chew. Rinne's become one of my new friends and knows I'm gay. But I haven't opened up about my past dating life and am definitely keeping what happened between Viktor and me under lock and key.

Especially since Viktor's shutting me out. He won't answer my texts or calls, avoided me like the plague at practice before we left. He's even calling me Coach Harper, and I fucking hate it.

I swallow the candy and stare out the window of the charter bus. "Something like that."

"Wanna talk about it? Not that I'm much help. Been out of the game for ten years."

I snort. "Lucky you. Not all of us are fortunate enough to marry our high school sweethearts."

He shoots me an incredulous look. "Don't even go there. Our relationship was some second chance romance level shit. Like it could be made into a TV drama."

My head tilts. "Really?"

He blows out a long breath. "Yup, one of those parents interfering and ruining our relationship. But it worked out in the end. Anyway, what's going on with you?"

"Psycho ex, and I met someone I like, but not sure I'm ready to jump into anything serious yet."

"Because you can control when the universe throws curveballs, huh? If that was the case, trust me, the births of my kids would've been better planned."

Ugh, he sounds like my brother. Tommy kept calling back after Viktor left, worried it had been Noah. My brother listened as I filled him in, then pretty much gave me the same speech.

I glance over the seat toward the back of the bus where Viktor's leaning against Knight because of course that's just who he had to sit with. What eats at me even more is the way he's blankly staring out the window, headphones on and hood pulled over his hat.

"Looks like you're not the only one with boy problems."

My heart rate spikes at the comment. "What do you mean?"

"He gets like this every now and then. Goes from that just started seeing someone giddiness to withdrawn and sad because he got dumped. Usually only lasts a day. But something's different this time."

My stomach twists. Rinne's words hit harder than I expected, making it difficult to breathe. Clearing my tight throat, I ask, "He said he got dumped?"

"Nah. Just seen the routine enough over the past three years. Think him and Knight even dated at one point. Glad they got over their shit."

I clench my teeth so hard they start to ache. And, of course, Knight glares right at me. So do Reed and Walsh.

Rinne looks in the same direction I do. "Gotta give it to them. They're all super protective of one another. Kinda jealous about it if I'm being honest. Wish I had a group of friends like that."

I face forward once again. "You want a bunch of entitled bullies as friends?"

"You telling me you wouldn't want rich friends? But nah, it's their loyalty, like they consider each other family. They accept each other regardless. I mean, fuck, while Novotny's a pain in the ass, I can't even imagine what Knight would be like without them."

Suddenly there's a commotion.

"Fuck off, man. Leave me alone."

We turn just as Knight kicks the back of the chair in front of him. Henneman's chair. Rinne and I are on our feet, moving down the aisle before a fight breaks out.

"Knock it the fuck off. Now!" My voice booms, low and threatening.

But Henneman ignores me and stands to face Knight. "Give it back!"

Rinne grabs him by the shirt, then pulls him toward the front of the bus, but he keeps fighting.

I face Knight, eyes narrowed. "What did you take?"

"Nothing."

"Give me whatever the fuck you took."

"Give it to him," Viktor says, continuing to stare out the window.

Knight hands over a beat-up small teddy bear. I take it, blinking a few times, then walk back to the front of the bus where Henneman now sits in my seat beside Rinne. I hand him the stuffed animal and he takes it, stuffing it into his jacket.

"It's my good luck charm." His eyes dart around and something tells me it might be more than that, but I don't push.

Rinne stands and faces the rest of the team. "You all have your little superstitions. Touch the bear again and I swear I'll rip Novotny's Ace of Spades card."

Viktor jumps out of his chair. "What the hell did I do? Don't you fucking dare touch my shit."

"Then tell your friends to stop fucking with Henneman. And, as for your card, if I destroy your good luck charm it affects the team, being you're our top goalie. So it would be in everyone's best interest to leave the fucking bear alone. Am I understood?"

They all mumble and he sits back down. Next to us, Nieminen is laughing. "Damn, Rinne. Using inside information on Novotny to get them in line. See, Harper, sometimes with these little shits you gotta play outside the lines. But you know that already."

Something about the look he gives causes me to squirm.

With Henneman in my seat, I have no choice but to take his, which means sitting next to the four Titans who want to rip my head off. Well, three of them do. Not sure where Viktor's head is at.

The rest of the ride to Penn State is quiet, thank God. I even take a little nap. When we pull up to the rink, everyone disembarks, making their way inside.

Or so I think.

Because the next thing I know, I'm being dragged behind the bus, then slammed up against it.

Knight, Walsh, and Reed crowd me, their eyes narrowed and lips pressed into thin lines.

"You wanna go at me, threaten me if I touch him? You made him sad. I fucking swear I even saw tears. You made him cry!" Knight's fist tightens around my jacket.

"Jeez, Coach. What did you do to him?" Reed eyes me, waiting for an answer.

While I should be angry, scared even, all I can think about is what Rinne said earlier and how it would be nice to have friends that cared this much.

"You hurt him? Do something you shouldn't have? Do we need to make you disappear too?" Walsh smirks as he says it. "I'm sure Buckland would like some company."

My eyes widen as I inhale sharply. They killed their former coach.

Holy shit.

Knight snorts. "Looks like he's finally getting with the program."

"Let him go."

I don't need to look to see who it is. But the barely-there tone is like a stab in the chest. When I do turn, Viktor's eyes are downcast. "Viktor?"

He still avoids my gaze and faces his friends. "We need to warm up."

The four of them head off toward the rink and I stare after them—after him—hoping he'll turn around. But he doesn't.

I rake my hands through my hair, tugging at the roots, regretting ever mentioning us being casual because no matter how logical it would be, we're not.

Now I just have to figure out how to fix this.

Viktor

CHAPTER SIXTEEN

One thing about having an obsessive personality, I'm able to pivot what I'm intensely focused on. It's how we beat Penn State. While my heart wasn't in the game, I defaulted to my more negative trait as some people like to call it.

But how can it be so bad if my obsession with being the best actually makes me so. And that's not me being narcissistic—my stats prove it. So does the fact the Islanders keep inquiring if I'll reconsider leaving school early.

Answer's always going to be no.

I want to finish my degree.

Our win wasn't all just me. Henneman stepped up, came out of his shell. Sure, he doesn't fight, not the way the rest of the team does. But he's a fucking good defenseman.

The Titans may just be a mismatch for him.

I also caught the way he checked in with Rinne a few times, which means some sort of conversation happened.

Not that I need the help. Me and my lucky card are perfectly capable of defending the net.

Taking out my wallet, I rub my thumb over the edges of the burnt Ace of Spades, then make sure it's tucked away securely before putting my wallet back into my pocket. If only the card would bring me luck in every area of my life.

My phone dings and I pull it out. Opening my email, I glance over the message from our family lawyer confirming receipt of the signed contracts. Good. At least Mouse will be safe. No one gets to fuck with that little princess anymore.

Walking across the parking lot to the McLaren, I breathe in the cold air. Figure I'll take a ride over to my parents and hang out with them for the weekend. Hopefully, my twin sister's done some stupid shit again that might cheer me up, especially if it's something that gets Dad all riled up.

While I may be a headache, she brought some old guy home and had him fuck her on the dining room table just as my parents came back from dinner a few years ago. Then she looked straight at my father and gave him the finger. Payback—as she called it—for our dad not sticking up for her after finding out Mom was sending her to live with my aunt to learn more about the family business.

Can't believe I missed it, but my ass was busy at goalie camp.

Just as I open the passenger side door on the McLaren to toss my shit inside, the roar of a familiar engine catches my attention. Beckett pulls up beside me, revving his bike, the sound echoing in my chest.

He lifts the visor of his helmet, his two different colored eyes boring into mine with an intensity that makes my heart skip a beat. "Get on."

"No."

He hurt me. Used information I shared with him, information about a vulnerable part of myself, and fucking hurt me with it.

Even Jackson got concerned when I came home, my eyes watery and puffy after Beckett told me he finds the idea of a relationship with me *too much*.

He called Eli, who showed up wearing Alexei's shirt. Like who didn't see that coming?

It was kinda funny when Jackson got annoyed his two blond friends were moping around in their boyfriends' clothes.

Only Beckett's not my boyfriend.

"Get on, now." Beckett's voice is low, demanding, as he grabs my arm, pulling me closer. But I yank free, taking a step back.

"Leave me alone."

We stand, staring at one another, the tension between us as thick and suffocating as a vat of molasses in January. I'm not sure why he's here, or what he even wants.

But I do know for once I'm done convincing him to be with me. I want someone to choose me and all my too muchness on their own.

"Chaos, please. I was wrong." His voice softens, almost pleading, and something in my chest tightens.

"Yeah, you were."

But so was I, because while I may want Beckett to be mine, he never said he was. I just assumed and then reality slapped me in the face.

"Please, get on the bike." His voice trembles, and it tugs at something deep inside.

"Fine."

As I throw my stuff into the car and lock it, Beckett gets the foot pegs in place. I climb on, placing one of my hands on the tank and grabbing my wrist with the other hand, my body instinctively leaning into his.

He pulls his visor down, then we're off. It's too cold to be riding, and I have no idea why this airhead doesn't own a regular car, or why we didn't take my car to wherever the fuck we're going.

Doesn't matter, not really, because I miss being this close to him.

When we pull up to his apartment, I'm relieved. Mostly because I can't stop shivering. Seriously, this idiot needs to buy a regular car.

Once inside, I take off my sneakers and just stand there, hands in the pockets of my jeans.

Beckett grazes his thumb across my cheek. "Fuck, you're cold. Come here."

He pulls me against him, then wraps his arms around me before lifting me and walking to the couch. He sits with me still in his lap, then grabs the throw blanket and drapes it across us both.

"I'm not a child."

"Sure about that?"

I sit up, eyes narrowed. "Really? You—"

"Stop. I was just trying to make a joke. Obviously, it was in poor taste."

"No shit."

He sighs and holds my gaze. "I'm sorry."

"You shouldn't have to apologize for how you feel. I was being overdramatic because I didn't get what I want." When he blinks a few times, his mouth opening and closing like a dumb fish, I roll my eyes. "I'm self-aware enough to know how I act, even if I choose to continue doing so."

"Not sure how to respond to that."

"Look, I'm fucking beautiful, extremely smart, and filthy fucking rich." I shoot him my best flirty-with-a-side-of-devilish smile. "But I'm also insane, overdramatic, and entitled. Seems no one can handle the combo. It's not a new revelation or anything."

"You left out the part where you don't listen very well. None of this was about you. Otherwise, I would've steered clear after you smashed that guy's face into the mirror at the gala."

"Nooo. I was your knight in shining armor, defending your honor. He touched you."

Beckett chuckles. "I remember."

When he pulls me back against him, I go willingly, melting into his chest as he adjusts the blanket. "I was wrong. I thought I needed casual, and it would make sense until I'm settled. But I haven't slept since that night. I'm fucking miserable."

I nuzzle into him, my heart beating erratically, yet I feel calm at the same time. "Me too."

Of all the partners I've had, none have ever cuddled with me. Sure, some did the aftercare bullshit, but it just came across too technical. And this just feels too fucking good, like I can barely keep my eyes open.

Except it all finally hits me.

Holy shit.

I push off him and look into his eyes. "Are you saying you want to be my boyfriend?"

Beckett laughs so hard, the boom of the sound reverberates through me, filling the room. "Wow, for someone so smart, took you long enough to figure it out."

"How do you know how smart I am?"

"Read your transcript. On track to graduate Summa cum laude."

"Damn right. Now back to the boyfriend thing. How's it going to work, you know with your job?"

He leans in and places a soft kiss on the tip of my nose. "Let's just get through the season, keep it to ourselves, and then we can figure it out over the summer. You only have one more year before you graduate."

"So . . . secret relationship?"

He eyes me, brows furrowing. "It's not ideal, but for now, yes."

I let out a loud groan. "This would've been so awesome if Jackson didn't have a better secret relationship story."

Beckett burrows his head into my neck, nipping and kissing me. "You're jealous your friend has a better story about hiding who he was dating? You're ridiculous."

"No one's ever called me that before. But if you kiss me every time you say it, I might end up liking it."

He chuckles, then grabs my chin, pinning me with a serious stare. "One more thing. We do this, then no more flirting with other people, whether it's in front of me or not. I catch you so much as batting those pretty blue eyes at someone else, I'll make damn sure you regret it."

I quirk a brow. "Wow, Becks. Didn't know you were so possessive."

"You have no idea." He pats my ass. "Now, get up. Time for a shower."

"What? Why? I took one before we left Pennsylvania."

"Because you don't smell like me anymore."

Oh.

That's what he meant about not all markings having to be physical. Sneaky fuck. He's been scent marking me.

Beckett

CHAPTER SEVENTEEN

Viktor stands at the edge of my bed, staring down at the toys on the mattress. I try to gauge his reactions, making sure to watch each and every movement no matter how slight.

"Never knew you were into this kind of stuff, Becks. What's next, gonna take me to a dungeon?"

"Not into that scene anymore."

His head snaps up, eyes wide. "Wait, you . . ."

I nod. "Lived it for a bit after my injury, experimented before then. But in the end, while I learned a lot, I'd rather just have someone at home to play with. And not all the time."

He chews on his bottom lip, then takes a deep breath. "Was Noah into this stuff?"

I've been waiting for him to bring my ex up again. Am kind of surprised it's taken this long, knowing his obsessive personality, though I've also been worried about what he might be doing on his own.

"Yes, it's how we met." I sit and pat the space beside me, and when he settles in, I continue. "Noah's a sub, like a full-time sub. I hated my life after tearing my back muscle and not being able to return to the NHL, hated my boring-ass job, so it was all exciting at first."

Viktor remains quiet, which is odd, but his shoulders are relaxed, his focus on me. No sign of distress, more like he's interested.

"Eventually, I figured out it wasn't for me. Noah didn't take it well. He tried to manipulate me to change my mind. When we broke up, he lost his shit. I should've done it somewhere public instead of at my house. That's when he hurt Mouse. You know the rest."

His lips press into a thin, hard line. "That dumb fuck will pay for what he did to my little princess."

My jaw drops and then I laugh. I know I shouldn't but I can't help it. "So, Mouse is yours now?"

"Fuck yeah, I didn't just . . ."

My eyes narrow when he stops. "You didn't just do what, Viktor?"

He huffs. "Don't make a big deal and freak out okay?"

My body goes perfectly still, and I breathe slowly and deliberately, trying to remain calm because internally I feel like a tornado siren just sounded. "What did you do?"

He smirks, scratching his head. "I kinda bought the building."

"Which building?"

"This one."

His response is like a blast of air launching me across the room. I'm dumbfounded, at a loss for words except for one. "Why?"

"Uh, because you snuck a cat into a no pets allowed building, dumbass. And my princess deserves to be safe." He crosses his arms in front of his chest. "Thought you of all people would've done a better job protecting her."

Fucking hell.

"And now that I'm your new landlord I never want to hear any shit about power dynamics. Yeah, you only mentioned it once, but guess what. I own the place you live. Therefore, I hold way more cards than you do, Coach Boyfriend."

As hard as I fight it, I'm smiling so wide my cheeks hurt. This chaotic demon purchased a building to protect my cat. "Please don't call me Coach Boyfriend again."

The evil smirk that appears as he straddles my lap has me worried. "Then maybe we should stop talking and we can get to using some of these toys."

My lips press against his, my tongue invading his mouth, wrestling for dominance. "Tell me exactly what you want, Chaos."

"Fuck me so hard I can still feel you tomorrow."

Lifting his shirt over his head, I throw it onto the floor, then deepen the kiss as I flick and pinch his nipples. I kiss my way down his chest and bite the hard buds, rolling my tongue over each one as I clasp them between my teeth.

Viktor whines, grabbing at my hair, hips rutting against me.

After a few seconds, I pull away and reach across the mattress to grab the first toy, holding the clips attached to a chain up. "Yes or no?"

"Fuck yes. Yes, now. Put the clamps on me now. Becks, please."

"Jesus fucking Christ." I swear he's about to rip the nipple clamps from me and put them on himself. "So needy, Chaos."

He hisses when I attach the first one, but it's quickly followed by a moan. Same with the second, and when I pull gently on the chain his eyes roll back into his head as his body shivers.

"Stand up and remove your pants. Underwear too."

He does and when the joggers drop, I moan, my cock throbbing at the sight of the huge wet spot on his blue boxers which is growing by the second. When he's completely naked, I slick his length with some lube, then slide the cock ring on, stroking him once right after.

Grabbing the set of leather cuffs, I stand, then step behind him. "I'm going to bind your hands and ankles and then I'm going to fuck you until my cock doesn't ache anymore."

"Do it. Fuck me into oblivion."

I kneel and kiss the back of his left thigh before wrapping the leather thigh cuff around and tightening it. I do the same with the other leg.

"How does that feel? Too tight?"

"It feels good," he says, voice breathy.

Next, I secure the ankle cuffs. Once they're on, I stand and pepper his back with kisses before placing each of the leather wrist cuffs on.

He looks at me, those ice blue eyes already growing hazy. "I'm so fucking hard, Becks."

I gently turn his head to face the mirror. "Look at how obscene your cock looks. How red and swollen it is. How much it's leaking."

When he whines, I tug the chain connecting the nipple clamps and his hips buck, cock drooling. He's panting and moaning, his own reflection turning him on.

"On the center of the mattress, face down, knees to your chest with your wrists at your ankles."

He crawls onto the bed and gets in position. I clip the double-ended snap hooks, connecting his right ankle and wrist to the D-ring of his right thigh cuff, then do the same to the left side. After, I grab the spreader bar and attach it to his ankles.

"How does it feel?"

"Like I'm about to come."

I slap his ass and he groans. "Are you okay being restrained in this position, smartass? Your knees okay?"

"Yes, but my fucking asshole needs attention. Please, Becks. Fuck me already."

I swat him again, harder this time and his whole body jolts. Placing my hand on his ass, I squeeze the pinkened flesh.

"That all you got, Becks?"

Oh, the brat's coming out to play, so the swats come faster, in quick succession, each time his body rocks forward a bit, the head of his cock rubbing against the sheets.

"Fuck, harder, Becks, please. Fuck, more. Please!"

I laugh a little and stop, reaching under him to tug on the nipple clamp chain. He wails and pulls at the cuffs, rubbing his face into the mattress.

"Viktor, do you need to stop?"

"No!" He looks back at me, tears staining his cheeks. "Please, don't stop."

Taking my time to undress, I watch as he squirms and mumbles to himself. Reaching into my nightstand, I grab a condom, then put it on before slicking myself up.

"Ready?"

"Y-yes. Fuck me. Own me."

I lean over, kissing down his spine and over his heated cheeks before lapping at his hole, sucking it, and tasting him to loosen him. Once he's ready, I line myself up, then push inside with one hard thrust.

"Becks!" He tries to move, to swivel his hips but he can't. Viktor's completely at my mercy.

I drive in so deep, there can't be a place I don't touch. I want to fuck him so hard it's branded on his soul who he belongs to.

"You look so pretty with my cock stretching you open. And you feel so good. So fucking tight and hot." My body is slick with sweat, and the room fills with the sounds of our ragged breathing and the rhythmic slap of skin against skin.

I take in Viktor's reflection in the mirror. His face contorts in pure ecstasy, tears streaming down his cheeks.

"Becks, please, I need to come."

"Not yet." I lean over, my chest to his back, and rut him harder, reaching underneath to tug on the nipple clamp chain. "You're mine, Viktor. Say it."

He whimpers, his body trembling. "I'm yours."

"Louder. I want to hear you scream it."

"I'm yours! Only yours!"

My body's on fire, but it's more than that. The way he's taking me, trusting me . . . I don't want anyone else.

Ever.

Heat burns me from the inside out, my thrusts erratic as I slam into him over and over. Reaching underneath, I grip his length firmly, stroking him fast and hard.

"Come with me, baby. Come with me," I say, my voice hoarse with desire.

Viktor's body tenses, and with a final, powerful thrust, we both shatter. His cries mix with my own, the intensity of our release leaving us both breathless and spent.

Slowly, I pull out, careful not to hurt him. Viktor's body is limp, his breathing steady and eyes closed. I reach out and brush a lock of hair from his forehead, smiling softly as he leans into my touch.

"Let me get you out of these," I murmur, reaching for the restraints.

I carefully unclip each snap hook, and he sighs in relief, his body relaxing further as I remove all the leather cuffs.

"Are you okay?" I ask, my voice gentle, scanning his face for any signs of distress.

He nods, his eyes still closed. "Yeah. More than okay. Do you always play like that?"

I press a kiss to his forehead, then his nose, and finally to his lips. "Not always. You handled it well."

After cleaning us up, I grab one of my sweatshirts from the closet and help put it on him before I climb under the covers, pulling him close, knowing with every fiber of my being this is the way every night should end, that he is my end.

Beckett

CHAPTER EIGHTEEN

The crisp autumn breeze nips at my cheeks as I step out of the Uber, its coolness a stark contrast to the warmth of the car's interior. I pull my jacket tighter, shielding from the chill while balancing the weight of the groceries in my arms as I stride toward my apartment.

I love the days where we only have practice once. It gives the players time to recover, but also affords me time to do things like cook dinner for Viktor. While we're careful to keep our relationship hidden, I still want it to be more than fucking all the time.

And he needs this.

My cocky, infuriating, beautiful brat needs to know he's special.

Not to mention, I'm falling for him. Fast and hard, like a puck to the head. And it scares the hell out of me. It helps that Mouse has taken a liking to him. The sassy cat may hiss and yowl, but she purposely seeks him out too.

Tommy's even happy about it. Though I can't really tell if my brother's happy I'm dating, happy I'm not letting

Noah run my life anymore, or just living vicariously through me since he's struggling to find someone.

Once upstairs, I fumble for my keys, juggling the bags. I should have about two hours until Viktor's class are over. But the moment I enter the kitchen, any sense of joy is squashed.

Sitting at my kitchen table like a nightmare come to life is Noah. And restrained in his arms, squirming and growling, is Mouse.

The bags slip from my suddenly numb fingers, food spilling onto the floor. But I barely register the mess at my feet. All I can focus on is my psycho ex-boyfriend, in my home, clutching my cat, a cruel sneer twisting his lips.

"What the fuck are you doing here?" My voice is low and seething. "How did you even get in?"

Noah just smiles serenely, like this is some pleasant social call and not a violation of the court order meant to keep him the hell away. "Hello, Beckett. Miss me?"

My hands curl into fists at my sides, blunt nails biting into my palms. It takes every ounce of my rapidly fraying control not to vault across the room and beat that smug look off his face.

Mouse's yowling intensifies, and Noah's grip on her tightens, making her wheeze.

"Let her go."

Noah clicks his tongue. "We used to be so close, you and I, before you got this thing and then threw me away like yesterday's trash."

"You cut her ear off. Now let her go, and get the fuck out of my apartment. We're over. Done. Accept it and move the fuck on."

He scoffs, rolling his eyes. "Move on? You're mine, Beckett. You've always been mine. No piece of paper is going to change that."

Unease prickles up my spine at the crazed glint in his eyes, the manic edge to his smile. I knew he was obsessed but this?

"You're violating the restraining order. Do you understand that? If you don't leave immediately, I'm going to call the police."

He barks out a sharp laugh. "Oh, that's rich. You'd really send me to jail? After everything we've been through?"

"Without hesitation."

An ugly sneer twists his mouth. "Oh, I'll leave. But you're coming with me. I'll make you see, make you understand. We belong together."

"Like hell."

Noah's mouth parts to say something, but the sound of my front door opening cuts him off. We both whip around. Viktor strides into my apartment like he owns the place, his backpack swinging from one hand.

He stops short at the sight of us, brows furrowing. "Who's this asshole?"

Noah rises to his feet, still gripping Mouse tightly. He looks Viktor up and down with a contemptuous sneer. "Ah, you must be the slut Beckett's been screwing around with these days. Gotta say, I'm not impressed."

Viktor steps into the kitchen, placing his bag on the counter while meeting Noah's disdainful gaze head-on. "And you must be the discount bin Robert Pattinson knockoff ex I've heard so much about."

"Enough!" My booming voice cuts through the rising tension, then I point a shaking finger at Noah. "Get out. Now. I won't ask again."

"Not without you." He takes a step back and pulls a knife from his pocket, pressing the sharp blade to Mouse's throat. She thrashes in his grip, her little body shaking.

"Noah, stop!" I roar, my heart in my throat. "You're hurting her!"

He tenses, a manic glint in his eye. "You did always love this stupid animal more than anything else."

I brace myself for him to lash out. But he jukes to the side and sprints for the door, shoving past me and bolting out of the apartment with Mouse clutched to his chest.

Viktor takes off after him, and I'm right behind. We thunder down the stairs, our shoes slapping against the concrete. Bursting out of the front door, we turn the corner just in time to catch Noah darting across the street, cars honking and tires screeching as he dashes between them.

And then, in one heart-stopping moment of unthinkable cruelty, he turns to face us, then hurls Mouse into oncoming traffic before rushing off.

Viktor doesn't hesitate. He sprints right into the road, dodging blaring horns and screeching tires. My heart stops as he snatches up Mouse a split second before a delivery truck comes barreling toward him, brakes squealing.

"Viktor!"

Sheer adrenaline propels me forward and I tackle him out of the way, a hair's breadth from the truck's grill. We hit the asphalt hard, rolling to the curb in a tangle of limbs, my body folded protectively around him.

"Are you okay?" My hands frantically skim over him, checking for injuries. "Are you hurt?"

"No, I'm fine. Except you're squashing us and she's clawing at me. Mind getting up?"

But when I try to stand, white-hot agony lances through my back and I drop back to one knee, groaning.

It's enough room for Viktor to scoot out from under me. "Shit, Becks. Your back."

"I'm fine," I grit out stubbornly, even as sweat beads on my brow from the pain. "Nothing ibuprofen and muscle relaxers won't fix. Let's just get inside. Get Mouse checked over."

A handful of people who've pulled over help me to my feet, asking if we're okay. Someone asks if she should call 911, but Viktor waves her off.

Slipping an arm around my waist, he helps support my weight as we make our unsteady way back to my apartment.

Instead of the stairs, we take the elevator, the ride a painful blur. We barely make it through my front door before my knees give out and I collapse onto the couch.

Distantly, I'm aware of Viktor puttering around, opening and shutting cabinets before he's back at my side, pressing a glass of water and some pills into my hands. "Here. Take these."

I toss them back and drain the glass, collapsing against the cushions. Viktor settles next to me, reaching out to stroke Mouse, who's curled up on my chest, still shaking like a leaf.

As the meds kick in and exhaustion starts to drag me under, I roll my head to study Viktor's profile. Even now, with his hair a wild mess, he's breathtaking. The afternoon light filtering in through the windows gilds his finely boned features, his pale hair glowing like a halo.

Fuck.

He really is my knight in shining armor.

"Love you, Chaos."

He glances at me, one eyebrow arched, but something bright and fragile kindles to life behind his eyes. "You don't have to say that just because I was almost roadkill . . ."

"I'm not." Lifting my heavy hand, I cup his cheek. "Seeing that truck coming at you . . . I've never been so fucking scared in my life. The thought of losing you . . ." I swallow thickly, emotions clogging my throat. "I love you. I'm so fucking in love with you it terrifies me."

His eyes widen, lips trembling, like he's almost afraid to believe me. And then, like a sunrise breaking over the horizon, a wide, stunning smile lights up his face. "Knew I could make you fall in love with me."

Such a fucking brat.

But he's mine.

My beautiful, brave, chaotic brat.

He turns into my palm, pressing a fierce kiss to the center. "I love you too, you gigantic, grumpy asshole."

While I want to kiss him, the longer I fight to stay awake, the more the world spins, so I close my eyes. The last thing I feel before I succumb are his lips grazing my ear as he says, "Don't worry, Becks. I'll handle Noah."

Viktor

CHAPTER NINETEEN

The door of my McLaren slams shut behind me with a satisfying thunk. I stride past the guards at the entrance of our family's abandoned factory, their deferential nods barely registering. Normally, I'd make some kind of spectacle of myself, maybe blow them a kiss or two just to see them squirm.

But not today.

I slip my psycho nun mask on as I make my way inside, the sleek crystalline material molding to my face like a second skin. It's my armor, my cape. When I wear it, I feel like the motherfucking Batman of murder.

I pause to double-check the bandage on my hand before tugging on leather gloves. Mouse just had to bite me earlier today when I tagged her.

Can't blame her, even Beckett winced in his drug-induced sleep when I injected the tracker into him. He was in so much pain, Urgent Care prescribed him some percs. So, when he took them with the muscle relaxer, my grumpy boyfriend was practically drooling in his sleep.

It was the perfect opportunity.

A pathetic whimper draws my attention to the man crumpled on the concrete floor.

Noah.

The cumstain should've left town, but instead he stayed, which made it easy to find him, especially when he stands out like a sore thumb in Rosewood Bay. Same way scholarship students do at Crestwood University. And the residents—yeah, if you don't belong, get the fuck out.

Mom got involved. Turns out, Mrs. Knight had been up the road when the piece of shit threw Mouse into the road. She saw the whole debacle and called my mother.

My parents called a mandatory family meeting, which led to me telling them I'm dating my coach. Their faces paled, my father growling as he asked which one. Kinda odd, more so when I revealed it was Beckett because they exhaled dramatically, their shoulders slumping as if relieved.

I told them about Noah and what he did, then Mom made a few calls and here we are.

Alexei's looming over him, a disgusted sneer twisting his lips. He draws his foot back and slams it into Noah's side, the sickening crack of breaking ribs echoing through the cavernous space.

Noah howls, curling in on himself like the spineless worm he is. I click my tongue, unimpressed.

"We're just getting started, bitch boy. You ain't seen nothing yet."

"This going to be quick or painful?" Alexei asks as I stand beside him.

I shoot him a sharp grin, all teeth. "Oh, he's gonna scream. That's a fucking promise."

Right now, the infamous Petrov bloodlust from my mother's side is singing in my veins, the beast inside howling for Noah's head on a fucking platter.

And who am I to deny it?

"Don't make this too long. I want to spend time with my Solnyshko."

"I could've handled this myself. You didn't have to come. I know Feisty Mouse is excited to see you."

"Family first always, you dumb fuck."

I snicker and look at him. "Yeah, how long before you officially make him family? You know you want to."

I catch the way his lip twitches upward. Yup, my cousin's definitely been thinking about marriage.

A pained groan from the floor reminds me that I've got more pressing matters to attend to. Namely, beating Noah's face in until it looks like roadkill pizza.

I crouch next to him, wrinkling my nose at the sharp stench of piss and terror. Fucking pathetic.

"Wakey, wakey, cumstain." I sing-song the words, tapping his bruised cheek none-too-gently. "Time to pay the fucking piper."

"Fuck you," he slurs, blood bubbling over his split lips. "You crazy fucking bastard. You won't get away with this, I'll—"

"Shh, sweetie. Now, since you're going to die anyway, I'm gonna give you a choice. Which hand do you want me to start beating you with, left or right?"

"P-please," Noah stammers, tears and snot mingling with the blood on his face. Disgusting. "Please don't. I'm sorry. I'm so sorry—"

"Didn't ask for a fucking soliloquy." I snarl, patience evaporating as I fist my hand in his hair, wrenching his head back. He yelps, scrabbling weakly at my wrist. "Left or fucking right, shitstain. I won't ask again."

"Left! Left, please, God—"

"There. Wasn't so hard, was it?"

My fist slams into his face, the crack of cartilage like a symphony as his nose shatters beneath my knuckles. He howls, high and thin, thrashing under me. The second punch collides with his cheek, the third to his eye socket. Each blow lands with satisfying crunches, the noise fueling my relentless assault.

"Okay, that's enough playtime, boys." My mother's cool voice cuts through the haze of violence, startling me out of my trance. I look up, chest heaving as she makes her way to us, the heels of her boots clicking against the concrete floor.

"Mom." I straighten up slowly, shaking out my aching hand. "Nice of you to join the party."

She pinches the bridge of her nose, looking skyward as if praying for patience. "Amateurs, the both of you. No technique, no finesse."

"Here we go."

Instead of just letting me kill this fuckhead, she's going to make it into a lesson. Because that's what she does. Not the teaching, the killing. And she's good at it. The best.

My cousin crosses his arms in front of his chest. "What is wrong with hitting this flea?"

She pokes Alexei in the chest. "You play for the NHL. My son will too. Why ruin your hands or your feet, risk breaking bones for no reason? It's not smart. Will your team not ask questions?"

I huff because she just has to make a valid argument.

"How'd you know Alexei was kicking him? I didn't see you when I pulled up?"

"Another reason you two need more training." My mother points to the far end of the open room. Right next to a beam is a camera just out of view. "Do not think just because we own a building that you are safe. You must always be diligent."

My cousin lets out a string of curses in Russian.

"Okay, okay, message received." I'm getting twitchy, my knuckles are itching to get back to rearranging Noah's face. "Can I get back to beating this motherfucker's ass now?"

She rolls her eyes and waves me on.

Crouching back down, I fish a pair of scissors from the pocket of my sweatshirt, then turn Noah's head sideways. He fights me, but Alexei uses his foot to hold his head in place.

"No more," he rasps, barely comprehensible. "Please, God. No more. I'm begging you—"

"You hurt my boyfriend. You hurt and disfigured my little princess. Think it's time you learn what it feels like."

Using the scissors, I cut off the top inch of his ear. It's not easy and he screams and writhes, but this is what he did to Mouse. I hum as I sit back on my haunches, twirling the gory flesh between my fingers, admiring the way the blood gleams. It's almost pretty, in a visceral sort of way.

"You should've stayed away. Then again, I would've tracked you down. And cut your ear off. Maybe I would've let you live." I look up at my cousin. "Open his mouth for me."

Alexei bends, then grabs Noah's jaw, wrenching it open. I drop the piece of his ear into it.

"Swallow."

Noah shakes his head, but Alexei holds his mouth closed and pinches his nose, cutting off his air until his Adam's apple bobs. Not wanting to breathe the same air as this fuck another moment, I drop the scissors and take out my knife from my back pocket.

Grabbing a handful of Noah's hair, I yank his head up before I slam the knife into his neck. His eyes bulge as his mouth flops open and closed like a fish before I rip out the blade, then stab him through the eye, twisting the knife in the socket. When I release his hair, his head hits the ground with a resounding thunk.

"Not bad. Making him eat his own ear, definitely something your father would have done," Mom says as Alexei helps me up.

My body vibrates, legs shaking a bit from the adrenaline coursing through my veins. Alexei walks with me to his bag in the corner of the room. We strip down and change our clothes, throwing the bloodied ones—including our shoes—into the bag.

Two guards come in and my cousin hands one of them the bag as we exit with my mother. The men will take care of Noah's body.

"You two are going to Russia this summer. You need to work on some of your skills."

We both nod. No point in arguing.

She heads off and Alexei and I walk to our cars. He pulls out his phone and taps on the screen, then looks up at me. "You coming to dinner or going to your boyfriend?"

"Honestly, I want to shower," I say, opening the door to my car and tossing the mask inside. "But dinner sounds good. Need to calm down."

Tomorrow is finally the start of our lives. Beckett is free. He no longer has anything to worry about.

Beckett

CHAPTER TWENTY

I can't believe this is happening. My life just seems to go from bad to worse. Leaning forward, I rest my head in my hands, the half-empty bottle of whiskey on the coffee table in front of me.

Fired. I've been fucking fired.

Though I'm not sure why it's coming as a shock. It was my choice to date Viktor, and I've always known it could come out. I was completely aware of the university's stance on relationships between staff and undergraduate students.

What I didn't expect were the photos President Ghoram slid across his desk in our meeting this morning. Photos of me and Viktor at the club. In the alley. In my bed.

All sent to the university by Noah.

He'd been in Rosewood Bay longer than I realized, watching me. Watching Viktor. My fingers curl into fists in my hair.

That sick fuck took my job, my reputation, my chance to stay in the world of hockey. And he almost took Viktor from me too. The image of my brat sprinting into traffic, that truck bearing down on him, is seared into my brain.

Groaning, I scrub my hand over my face. Fuck, I need a drink. Well, another drink.

As I reach for the bottle, my phone buzzes on the cushion beside me. I grab it, hope flaring in my chest. Viktor's been ignoring me, sending my calls to voicemail, leaving my texts unread.

But it's just Rinne, letting me know he's outside.

I'm really not up for visitors right now, but he's persistent.

Buzzing him into the building, I unlock the door, then drop back onto the couch.

"Hey, Harper," he says quietly, shifting his weight awkwardly. "How you holding up?"

I quirk a brow as I stare at him, lifting the bottle of whiskey.

"That bad?" He drops into the armchair across from me, then grabs the bottle, taking a swig. "Fuck. I needed that."

"Have the rest."

Rinne eyes me for a long moment, his gaze uncomfortably perceptive. "How's your back?"

"Feels like someone's taken a rusty hacksaw to my spine. But what else is new?" I snag the whiskey bottle back and take a long pull. The burn gives me something to focus on besides the throbbing ache radiating up my back.

Rinne's brow furrows. "You thinking about starting PT? Might help, you know. Get ahead of it before it gets worse."

I laugh, the sound bitter and brittle. "Sure, let me get right on that. It's not like I just lost my insurance along with my job or anything."

His mouth tightens, but he doesn't rise to the bait. "What about Viktor? Have you told him yet?"

Just the sound of my boyfriend's name makes my throat close up. I shake my head, blinking hard against the sudden sting in my eyes. "He's not returning my calls or texts. I don't . . . Fuck, Rinne. I'm worried about him."

"He skipped practice yesterday. And today." There's something in his voice, a note of hesitation that makes my stomach clench.

"What?"

He sighs, rubbing the back of his neck. "The Titans have a certain way of handling their business. Think Viktor went after your ex."

I swear, the day of the incident he mentioned something about taking care of the problem, but the drugs had hit me hard. Thought I imagined it.

Except Walsh made it clear they killed their former coach, the one who'd assaulted Reed.

"What if something happened to him? What if he's not answering because of Noah . . ." The words die off, my throat closing up.

Rinne grabs my shoulder, squeezing it. "Don't think that's the case, otherwise the rest of the three would be MIA as well. You really love him, don't you?"

I look up, staring at him incredulously. "Of course I fucking love him! Was the part where I threw myself in front of a truck for him not a big enough clue?"

Rinne barks out a laugh. "Easy, tiger. I was just asking."

"I love him so much it scares the shit out of me sometimes. The kid's a fucking chaotic hurricane. Blows into my life and just . . . upends everything. But I can't imagine my world without him in it anymore."

"For what it's worth, I think you're good for each other. But I gotta admit, I'm not sure how you deal with his . . . eccentricities. Not sure I can take all that obsessive bullshit myself."

While Rinne may be my friend, I want to slam my fist into his nose. "That obsessive personality makes him who he is. I thought you of all people would've noticed. He's a once in a generation goalie. Fucking amazing. But rough around the edges."

Rinne listens, face scrunching as if trying to fit the pieces together.

"Don't tell me you haven't seen that same obsessiveness applied to his training to chasing after perfection as a goalie."

My friend's brows raise high, mouth opening. "Fuck. Never thought of it that way."

"He's got a near perfect GPA in goddamn Chemical and Molecular Engineering." I can't stop the proud smile that spreads. My brat is not just brilliant in the net, he's just motherfucking brilliant.

"I get it. But what makes him great in certain areas of life, doesn't work for relationships."

My lips press into thin a line, nostrils flaring. "He's mine and it works for us. Talk shit some more and you'll be going home with a fat lip."

Rinne chuckles, but it dies quickly. "In all seriousness, though—how do you think he's gonna take the news? About you getting fired? You know he's going to retaliate somehow."

Understatement of the fucking century.

We sit there for a while, just talking, more Rinne listening as I vent. Eventually, he heaves himself out of the chair. "Gotta get home, but let me see what I can do to help. I'm sure I can get something out of Reed."

"Thanks."

He waves over his shoulder and then the door clicks shut softly behind him.

Snagging my phone off the cushion, I dial Viktor for the hundredth fucking time. It goes straight to voicemail.

Again.

"Listen, you stubborn chaotic shit. Call me back or get your ass to my apartment within the hour or I swear to God, Viktor, I will bend you over my knee and spank you center ice in front of the entire team."

I hit end too quickly, realizing after the fact who I just left that message for.

If anything, my demon brat won't be calling me back because I just threatened him with a good time.

Fuck my life.

Viktor

CHAPTER TWENTY-ONE

Sitting in one of the chairs on the other side of President Ghoram's desk, I pick at a loose thread on my designer jeans. When the door opens, I glance up, a smirk tugging at my lips as my mother strides in like she owns the place. Her Louboutins click on the hardwood, her gray suit perfectly tailored.

She perches her sunglasses atop her sleek updo, shooting a razor-sharp smile at my head coach. "It's been a long time, Coach Nieminen. Almost didn't recognize you with your clothes on."

Wait, what?

My head whips around so fast I nearly give myself whiplash, my gaze bouncing between her and Coach like I'm watching a tennis match. When did she see him naked? Unless . . . No fucking way!

I burst out laughing, doubling over in my chair. Rinne, who's standing next to me, scrunches his face up like a confused pug.

"Seems the Titans' coaches enjoy sticking it to my children," Mom says as she slides into the seat next to me.

Oh, man. This is gold. I always wondered why my dad looked like he was seconds away from strangling Nieminen, who, at the moment, looks like he wants the floor to swallow him whole.

Ghoram loudly clears his throat, annoyance etched into every line of his doughy face. "If we could please focus on the matter at hand . . ."

Everyone turns to face the older, thickset man. He steeples his sausage fingers, beady eyes narrowing. "Mrs. Novotny, your son set fire to my car. Not only was this destruction of property, but he put others in danger. Students and staff could've been seriously hurt. As it is, those who were in the immediate vicinity have some respiratory issues."

I roll my eyes so hard it hurts. "Oh, please. It was barely a campfire."

My mother ignores me, appearing calm as always. "What is it you want, Mr. Ghoram? The police have not arrested him, so what is it you're after?"

The older man sits straighter, puffing out his chest. "We all know when it comes to eighty percent of the student population, going to the police will do nothing, not with the lawyers you have at your disposal. What I want is

Viktor gone, expelled from the university and from the hockey team."

"Whoa, whoa, whoa. Expel me?"

"You're a menace. One that doesn't belong in my school."

I sit tall in the chair, spine straight, and shoot the bastard a matter-of-fact grin. "Let's all be clear here. I wasn't nearly as unhinged as I could've been, and you should all need to be thankful for that. Like, I could've barbequed him along with the car."

Rinne slaps me upside the head. "Not helping your case, dumbass."

"Well, he shouldn't have fired—"

My mother holds up her hand, cutting me off. "Viktor will face consequences. But expulsion is off the table. Surely, we can come to an agreement."

Nieminen clears his throat, then steps forward. "We need him on the team. He was an integral part in this university winning the championship last year."

"Coach Nieminen, this university has had enough issues with the hockey team lately. Between the coaches and the players, and from what I just overheard, you seem to have broken the university rules as well."

"Wrong, fucktard. My sister doesn't go here."

Water splashes onto my hand, Rinne coughing and choking behind me. "Your sister?"

I quirk a brow with a huge grin plastered on my face. "Oh, yeah. It's a hell of a story. I'll fill you in later."

Mom slaps the back of my head this time, her glare promising retribution. "You. Mouth shut. Now."

I mime zipping my lips, but I can't quite wipe away the smirk.

President Ghoram's looking more apoplectic by the second, his ruddy face verging on purple. "Mrs. Novotny, your son—"

She drums her blood-red nails on the armrest, the rhythmic tapping making Ghoram twitch, leveling him with an icy stare. "Let me stop you right there. You do remember who pays that fat salary you receive. Your wife has become accustomed to a certain lifestyle. It would be a shame for all of it to just go away."

Oh, snap.

But President Ghoram's not backing down. He leans forward, jabbing a finger in her direction. "And let me make myself clear. If you fight me on removing Viktor, I will press charges. I'll make his antics public, even to the NHL. I doubt any team will want to sign such a troublemaker, especially with his . . . dramatic proclivities."

I suck in a sharp breath. Is this asshole really threatening my future? Oh, I'll show him a fucking troublemaker—.

My mother's hand stills on the armrest. Uh, oh. I know that look, the one that precedes ruination.

I'm out of my chair and across the room before Ghoram can blink, pulling Rinne with me to the relative safety of the far corner. Nieminen, the brave bastard, doesn't move.

His funeral.

She rises from her seat with deadly grace, eyes locked on Ghoram like a shark scenting blood as she leans across the mahogany desk. "I don't take kindly to anyone threatening my children. So, here is what's going to happen. You will drop this nonsense about your car. And you will also reinstate Beckett Harper's job. Immediately."

"That man was having sexual relations with your son. This university prohibits all consensual relationships between faculty and undergraduate students, regardless of whether a faculty member has ever had teaching, evaluative, or other supervisory authority over the student. We believe that relationships between faculty and undergraduates are never truly consensual—even when both are adults—because of the inherent power differential."

Coach Nieminen pulls an iPad mini from his jacket, taps the screen, then places it on the desk before taking a step back.

The unmistakable sounds of two people going at it fill the room. Ghoram's eyes bulge as he stares at the screen, all color draining from his face.

Mom smiles, slow and shark-like. "While Beckett and my son are two consenting adults in a relationship, you bending your niece over this very desk is another matter entirely. Incest, I believe, is quite illegal in this state."

Holy shit.

Think my eyes are about to pop out of my skull, and Rinne looks like he's about to have an aneurysm.

"Fix this mess, Mr. Ghoram. Reinstate Beckett Harper and sweep that nasty car incident under the rug, or that video makes its way to the school board. And your wife," she says, voice dripping with false sympathy.

Ghoram's Adam's apple bobs as he swallows convulsively, a vein throbbing in his forehead. But I can see it in his eyes—he's beat and he knows it.

As the two hash out the details, Rinne elbows me in the side. I glance over at him, brows raised.

"You need to call him. He's freaking out."

My palm rubs over the center of my chest, trying to chase away the ache. I've gotten Beckett's messages and heard the worry in his voice. Well, except that last one.

That one made my dick hard.

"Once we're done here that's exactly where I'm going."

Rinne steps in front of me, his eyes hard, jaw set. "Listen to me. He loves you. Like really fucking loves you, Viktor. So, I swear to motherfucking God, this better not be some game where you toss him aside because you finally hooked him."

I narrow my eyes, trying to appear threatening, but I just end up smiling so hard my damn cheeks hurt. Mostly, because someone else is confirming how much Becks loves me, and while he tells me, there's something about hearing someone else say it that makes it real.

The other reason is because I'm happy my boyfriend has a friend willing to get in my face to protect him.

"Did you not see the Audi brûlée I created in the parking lot? It was a spectacle. People posting it got hundreds of thousands of views." I punch him in the shoulder. "I love him too, Coach. Not ever letting him go."

Not sure how much time passes, but eventually my mother jerks her head and I pop off the wall following her out. She pauses at the door to level one last imperious look at Ghoram. "I meant what I said about not taking kindly to people threatening my children."

She pulls out her phone and clicks on the screen a few times. "Good luck."

I scramble after her when she sweeps out of the office, wanting to know what she just did, even though deep down I already do. "Mom?"

"Come, time for me to meet this boyfriend of yours."

Beckett

CHAPTER TWENTY-TWO

Someone's pounding on the door like they're trying to break it down. I'm off the couch in a shot, heart hammering as I yank it open and there he is. My beautiful, infuriating brat.

"Sup, Becks," he drawls, sauntering past me into the apartment. "Miss me?"

I growl, hauling him into my arms before he can get another word out, crushing him to my chest, nose buried in his hair. He squeaks in surprise but melts into me instantly, his arms coming up to wrap around my waist.

I can't thank Rinne enough for shooting me a text he was with Viktor. Turns out, the chaotic demon did lash out over the university firing me. But that doesn't matter right now, not when he's finally here.

"You scared the shit out of me." I rasp into his hair, not even trying to hide the tremor in my voice. "I thought . . . Fuck, Viktor. I didn't know what to think when you wouldn't answer me."

"I'm sorry, okay? I had shit to handle."

Before I can mention the car bonfire he set, someone clears their throat behind him. When I look up, a blonde woman stares at me.

Viktor pulls back to give me a lopsided grin. "This is my mom. She wanted to meet you."

Fuck.

Meeting his mother is not how I saw this day going. I swallow hard, trying to wrangle my expression into something less gobsmacked as I straighten my shirt.

"Mrs. Novotny." I extend my hand. "It's a pleasure to meet you."

Her perfectly manicured hand grasps mine, her grip surprisingly strong. "Likewise, Mr. Harper. I've heard . . . interesting things about you."

There's a glint of something in her eye, a sharpness that makes me wonder exactly what she's heard. And from whom. But her smile seems genuine enough as she steps past me into the apartment.

I close the door, and when I turn, she's surveying the apartment, one brow arched. "Nice place. Cozy. Lots of potential. I can see why my son purchased the building."

I doubt Viktor was thinking about real estate investments. And I can't tell if her words are a compliment or a criticism.

She perches on the edge of the couch, ankles crossed primly. "I understand there was some . . . unpleasantness with your job, Mr. Harper."

I tense, my stomach twisting. "Yes, ma'am. I . . . I was fired."

She waves a dismissive hand, as if discussing the weather. "Not to worry. That's been handled. You've been reinstated, with a formal apology from the university forthcoming. Coach Nieminen will be reaching out to you shortly with the details."

I blink. Once. Twice. Three times. I must have misheard. "I . . . What?"

Viktor snickers, squeezing me tighter. "Mom verbally castrated Ghoram. It was epic."

"I . . . Thank you," I manage, my voice gruff with emotion. "Really. I don't know what to say."

Her gaze softens imperceptibly. "You're welcome. I know how happy you make Viktor. That's enough for me."

A sudden thought occurs and I turn to Viktor, brows furrowing. "Rinne texted me a few minutes ago. Did you set Ghoram's fucking car on fire?"

He blinks up at me, all wide-eyed innocence. "Um, define, 'set on fire'?"

"Chaos."

"Ugh, fine! Yes, I torched the dean's Audi. What was I supposed to do, send him a strongly worded email?"

I pinch the bridge of my nose, torn between throttling him and laughing. "You can't just go around burning people's shit when you're pissed. Two wrongs don't make a right."

He huffs. "Baby, I was making a point, not a right."

God, save me from stubborn, vindictive hockey players. But I can't quite stop the chuckle that escapes. "You're impossible. You know that, right?"

He grins, unrepentant. "You love me anyway."

"Yeah, I do."

Viktor releases me and drops down onto the couch next to his mom, then a flash of white in my peripheral vision catches my attention. Mouse is peeking out from behind the couch, her one blue eye and one green eye fixed on Viktor.

He glances over just in time to see her crouched, wiggling her little butt. A split second later, she launches herself at him with a mighty war cry.

"Shit!"

She latches onto his jaw, her teeth digging in before she starts aggressively licking his face, rumbling like a tiny chainsaw.

"Mouse, what the fuck!" Viktor sputters, trying to fend her off, but he's laughing, his eyes bright with joy. "I missed you too, you little demon."

"Like recognizes like." Mrs. Novotny continues to watch the two with an expression caught between amusement and bemusement. "Maybe I should've gotten him a cat growing up."

I glance at her. "He didn't have any pets growing up?"

She looks at me like I've sprouted a second head. "Have you met my son? His twin sister is even worse. I assure you, I did not have the bandwidth to add an animal to the mix."

I can only imagine the chaos of a house with not one, but two Novotny hellions running amok. "I didn't know he had a twin sister?"

Viktor finally manages to detach Mouse from his head, cuddling her to his chest. She purrs smugly, the little terror. "She's in Moscow with my aunt, learning the ropes of the family biz. You're in for a treat when you meet that hot mess."

"About that," Mrs. Novotny cuts in, pinning me with her stare. "Viktor will need to go to Russia for a few weeks this summer. I trust you'll be accompanying him? If you're serious about him, that is."

It's phrased as a question but feels more like a command. I straighten my spine, meeting her gaze head-on. "Yes, ma'am. I'll be there. And I'm in for the long haul. Your son . . . He means everything to me."

Her lips curve up, something like approval warming her gaze. But Viktor scoffs, rolling his eyes hard enough to strain something.

"Wait until you see what the family business is, Becks," he mutters, a sly grin playing about his mouth. "Might change your tune real quick."

"On that note, I should be going. I have a flight to catch." She levels one last look at me as she stands, her eyes glittering with some unspoken warning. "Take care of him, Mr. Harper. And the next time my son might be in danger, I expect you to notify me immediately. Are we clear?"

"Crystal."

She leans down to press a kiss to Viktor's hair, murmuring something in Russian. He nods, his expression uncharacteristically solemn. And then she's gone.

The second we're alone, I lunge at Viktor, pinning him against the cushions. My mouth crashes down onto his, my hands frantically roaming every inch of him, needing to feel him, to reassure myself he's here and whole.

"Don't you ever fucking scare me like that again." I rasp against his throat, my teeth grazing his jumping pulse. "I thought . . . I thought I lost you. Thought he'd gotten to you."

"As if." He tilts his head to give me better access, wrapping one leg around the back of my thigh. "He won't be a problem anymore."

I exhale a slow breath and pull back a bit. "Do I want to know?"

"Probably not."

"Your parents are going to hate me if whatever you did comes out. They'll blame me."

"Mom was there. She knows." His brilliant, icy blue eyes search mine, uncertainty flickering in their depths. "I really am sorry for worrying you. I couldn't let him fuck up your life anymore. You're my home, Becks. I protect what's mine."

I crush our mouths together once more, holding him so tight, he squeaks.

"Becks." Viktor sighs into my mouth, "I know I'm a lot to handle, but—"

"Shut up. You're perfect, you hear me? I love every wild, chaotic, batshit part of you."

His smile right now could rival the sun. "Then you better put a ring on it."

My heart damn near stops. But he's already trying to wriggle out from under me, his grin turning wicked.

"Think there's a message in my voicemail about getting spanked center ice." He looks down at that fancy blue watch of his. "Yup, I *definitely* didn't meet the time limit you gave."

"Fucking brat." But I'm laughing as I hoist him up and wrap his legs around me. "That smart mouth is gonna get you in trouble."

He slaps at my arms. "Wait, wait! Your back!"

I pinch his ass cheek, chuckling when he yelps. "My back won't be stopping me from tanning this ass for all the gray hairs you gave me."

"Looking forward to it, *Coach Harper*."

As I carry him to bed, both of us laughing, I feel it in my bones. This, right here?

It's forever.

Viktor

CHAPTER TWENTY-THREE

I can't stop giggling as Beckett kicks the bedroom door shut. The way he manhandles me, the casual show of strength, it never fails to get me hot. But I also keep an eye out for any wincing, any sign of pain that his psoas muscle is acting up.

"Think you're real cute, don't you?" He spins us so my back hits the wall. The impact punches a gasp out of me, but it quickly turns into a moan as he grinds against me, hard and insistent.

"I don't think. I know I'm fucking adorable. And you love it."

He hums, trailing biting kisses down the column of my throat. "Love this ass in my hands, that's for sure." He punctuates his words with a firm squeeze, pulling me flush against him. "Love the sounds you make when I'm buried deep even more."

Fuck.

I writhe against him, plucking at his shirt. "Then why are we still wearing clothes? Chop, chop, Becks. Get naked, come on."

He chuckles, lowering me to the ground, then strips off his shirt in one smooth motion. "Keep sassing me and you'll get it, brat."

"Oh, fuck yes. Yes, please."

I shimmy out of my clothes in record time, my skin tingling under the intensity of his gaze, heat pooling in my core as his eyes hungrily drink me in.

"Like what you see?" I smirk, cocking my hip.

A muscle in his jaw ticks, and his hands flex at his sides, like he's physically restraining himself from grabbing me. "Always, Chaos. Fuck, you're so gorgeous, you don't even know . . ."

A flush warms my cheeks. Hearing how much he desires me never gets old.

"Want me on my back so you can watch yourself split me open on your big cock? Or maybe you want me on my knees to pull my hair while you fuck my throat raw?"

Beckett makes a strangled sound, eyes flashing. In an instant, he's on me, one hand cupping my ass while the other tangles in my hair, tugging my head back.

"Tonight, I want to watch your face when your greedy hole swallows me up."

A shiver runs through my entire body, my hole clenching around nothing. "Holy shit. I think I just—"

He cuts me off with a kiss, licking into my mouth like he's trying to devour me. I cling to his shoulders, urging him back toward the bed until his knees hit the edge and he sits. I don't break the kiss as I straddle him, knees bracketing his hips, loving the way his breath hitches as I grind down.

"Lube." I gasp when we finally part for air. "And . . . ah, fuck . . . the clamps. Becks, please."

His grin is pure sin as he reaches into the nightstand. He tosses the lube on the bed but dangles the gleaming silver clamps from a finger. "These what you want, Chaos? Want me to put them on your pretty nipples, get 'em all red and aching?"

I can only nod frantically, skin already tingling in anticipation. The first clamp biting down makes me cry out, makes my back arch as the bright, hot pain zings straight to my dick.

The second one has me nearly sobbing, hips rolling mindlessly as I chase the intensity. Beckett groans, low and deep, hands stroking reverently over my sides.

There's the snick of the lube opening, followed by a slick finger circling my hole, and then he's pressing in. I gasp, bearing down eagerly, my nails digging into his shoulders. He works me open, crooking his fingers just right to graze my prostate.

By the time he's up to three, I'm panting, thighs trembling, sweat prickling along my hairline. "Fuck, Becks. Get in me. Fuck me."

He grabs the condom, tearing the foil packaging open. "Lift up."

I do, rising up on shaking thighs as he sheaths, then slicks himself. His blunt head presses against my hole and I sink down. It's so much, the stretch and the burn and the sweet ache of being filled. But I don't stop, I take him to the hilt until I'm fully seated on his lap, stuffed full of his cock.

"Fuck," Beckett grits out, fingers digging into my hips. "Fuck, you feel incredible, so hot and tight."

I can only mewl in response. He's so deep like this, filling me up, pushing the air from my lungs. I need a minute, need to—

Beckett thrusts up viciously, bouncing me on his cock. I wail, stars bursting behind my eyes as he hits my prostate dead-on.

"Oh, fuck." I gasp, head lolling back. "Oh, fuck. Becks, yes, yes, yes."

He moves at a relentless pace, fucking up into me hard and deep. And fuck, he's just as shameless, matching me cry for cry, growl for whimper. It's the hottest fucking thing I've ever seen.

And then he tugs the chain connecting the nipple clamps, sharp and deliberate. White-hot sensation sears through me and I keen, my back bowing. He does it again, timing it with a particularly brutal thrust, and I nearly fly apart.

"Wrap your hand around that pretty dick of yours and show me how well you can fuck your fist."

My hand leaves his shoulder, wrapping around my aching length. I fuck into the tight circle of my fingers urgently. It's graceless and sloppy and fucking perfect. "Fuck, gonna come. Fuck, fuck Becks. Oh, shit. Oh, shit. Oh, shit."

"Come for me, Chaos. Come on my cock."

And I do. I fucking detonate, thighs shaking as my orgasm crashes through me. Cum splatters over Beckett's chest and abs, coating my hand as I shake apart, spasming and clenching around him.

Distantly, I hear him curse, his fingers digging into my hips. He thrusts twice more and then he's coming too.

I collapse against his chest, boneless and spent. Beckett presses soft kisses to my hair, his hands stroking soothingly up and down my back.

Sweat is cooling on my skin and my ass aches, the nipple clamps a sweet, throbbing hurt. And I've never felt so utterly, completely content.

Beckett eases me off his softening cock and lays me out on the bed, removing the nipple clamps before disappearing into the bathroom. He returns with a damp cloth and cleans me up.

When he's done, he stretches out beside me, gathering me into his arms. I tangle our legs together, burrowing into his warmth. His fingers comb through my hair and I nuzzle into his chest.

"Love you," I mumble into his skin.

"Love you too, Chaos. Always."

I'm nearly asleep when something occurs to me. I crack an eye open, smirking up at his peaceful face. "We were pretty loud. Bet we sounded like a couple of pornstars going at it."

He snorts, not bothering to open his eyes. "What, you want a medal?"

I nip at his chest, grinning when he yelps. "Actually, I was thinking we should fuck in the president's office. Christen the desk for the next person."

The thing about my mom, she doesn't threaten, doesn't give second chances. You fuck up, you're done. Which is why she sent the video right as we walked out of the office.

Beckett groans, swatting me lightly on the ass. "You're a fucking menace, you know that?"

"But I'm your menace. No take-backs."

He huffs a laugh, arms tightening around me. "Wouldn't dream of it."

Viktor

CHAPTER TWENTY-FOUR

I settle into the crease, the familiar crinkle of my lucky Ace of Spades card tucked into my helmet. Cornell's offense is a well-oiled machine, cycling the puck with surgical precision. But I'm turning away shot after shot with acrobatic saves that leave the crowd gasping. Eat your heart out, Hašek.

Jackson wins the defensive zone face-off, sending it back to Henneman, who passes it right back and Jackson takes off. He streaks down the ice on a breakaway. It's a thing of fucking beauty, the way he undresses Cornell's defensemen with a filthy deke.

But when he shoots, Cornell's goalie snatches the puck out of the air like it's nothing.

"Fuck."

As the teams reset, I glance at the bench. Becks is watching, his jaw tight and his arms crossed. When our eyes meet, his expression softens. He shoots me a small nod and mouths, *Keep going. You've got this.*

And I do.

Cornell keeps crashing the net, but I'm a fucking fortress. Glove saves, pad saves, a sick fucking two-pad stack that leaves their forward looking like he's about to cry.

"Scoreboard, bitch!" I crow as he skates away, tapping my helmet mockingly.

But hockey's a fickle mistress, and she's not content to let me stay on my high horse for long. Early in the second, a seeing-eye shot from point finds its way through traffic and over my blocker.

Goddammit.

Their goon of a defenseman skates by, a smug grin on his punchable face. "What's the matter, Novotny? Puck knock the cock outta your mouth?"

Suddenly he falls over, groaning, and the ref's whistle blares.

Henneman stands over him but gives me a curt nod. When I look back down at the pissant, he's holding his cup. Well, fuck me. Quiet Henneman just high-sticked this fucker in the nads.

As our defenseman makes his way to the penalty box, Zach fist bumps him. About time my friend started treating the rookie like an actual teammate.

The rest of the period is a firefight, pucks zipping from end to end like tracer rounds. But neither team manages to find the back of the net. We head into the third tied at one.

"Just keep doing what you're doing, Novotny." Coach Nieminen growls, his gruff voice oddly soothing. "Give us a chance to win this fucking thing."

I nod, jaw set. I will. I fucking will.

Midway through the third, Jackson's cutting through the neutral zone, skating like the wind. But that fucking ogre who broke his ribs last season lines him up for a hit.

He misses, but they're fighting a second later.

And when Connor jumps in, it becomes an all-out brawl.

Not wanting to be left out, I smack my stick on the ice as I skate over the center line into their territory. "Come on, motherfucker."

Their goalie skates right at me and we start swinging, spitting curses and insults. Yeah, I remember the way he clapped when his teammate broke Jackson's ribs.

Someone screams my name, and someone is pulling at my jersey. But I don't stop, too busy trying to beat the ever-loving shit out of this asshole.

Eventually, we're pulled apart.

On the way back to the net, I smile wide at the bench. Becks just shakes his head while Rinne hides his face, his shoulders shaking. Yeah, of course he's laughing because goalie fights are rare. Bet he misses this shit.

After penalties are handed out, four players from each team in the box, the game gets back underway.

The minutes tick down and the score is still tied. I seriously don't want this game going into overtime. And definitely don't want a fucking shootout happening.

Henneman intercepts a pass. He's in their zone at the top of the end zone face-off circle. He takes a slapshot.

Please, please, please.

The horn blares.

"Fuck yeah!"

Game over.

In the locker room, chaos ensues. It's Henneman's first goal with the team and we're all celebrating. For once, he's smiling, even though his body is tense.

I make my way over, slapping his shoulder. "Way to go, Henny."

"Thanks."

Our coaches come in, giving a quick speech, then tell us to hurry the fuck up and get on the bus. Hands down, I'll be the last one out. But who fucking cares?

I look around. Maybe Becks and I can sneak in a quickie.

"You tell Coach yet about Miami?" Jackson asks.

"Working on that. Just gotta figure out how to tell him I'll be out of town for a few days. On a totally innocent, not-at-all-murder vacation with the boys."

"You're fucked," Zach says, not an ounce of sympathy in his voice.

Maybe I'll tell him while I'm riding him. Or choking on his dick.

I catch Becks' eye across the locker room, and he grins at me, slow and heated. It sends a shiver straight to my core, damn near buckling my knees.

Yeah. Definitely telling him in bed. And if that doesn't work . . . well. I'm sure I can come up with some other way to distract him.

After all, I'm the master of causing chaos. Might as well use my powers for good.

Or, at least, for a good dicking.

But hey, all's fair in love and maiming, right?

About the Author

E.V. OLSEN

E. V. Olsen is a romance author who loves to write about Over The Top alpha males who are possessive and completely obsessed with their person or mate. Nothing will get in their way from claiming what's theirs. She enjoys writing darker or angsty type romances whether in the contemporary world, PNR worlds, or even post-apocalyptic worlds.

Connect with E.V. Olsen online

EVOLSENBOOKS.WEEBLY.COM

TIKTOK.COM/@EVOLSENBOOKS

INSTAGRAM.COM/EVOLSENBOOKS

FACEBOOK.COM/EVOLSENBOOKS

Also By
E. V. OLSEN

Wasteland Temptations Series

Mine to Claim (Book 1)
Mine to Protect (Book 2)
His to Break (Book 3)
His to Lead (Book 4)

North Shore Titans Hockey Series

Savage Titan
Brutal Titan
Unhinged Titan
Forbidden Titan
Ruthless Titan